LIFE'S LITTLE DIFFICULTIES

Also by France Daigle

Real Life
1953: Chronicle of a Birth Foretold
Just Fine
A Fine Passage

LIFE'S LITTLE DIFFICULTIES

FRANCE DAIGLE

a novel

Translated by Robert Majzels

ANANSI

Copyright © 2002 Les Éditions du Boréal, Montréal, Canada
English translation copyright © 2004 House of Anansi Press Inc.

All rights reserved. No part of this publication may be
reproduced or transmitted in any form or by any means,
electronic or mechanical, including photocopying, recording,
or any information storage and retrieval system, without
permission in writing from the publisher.

First published as *Petites difficultés d'existence* in 2002 by Les Éditions du Boréal

Published in 2004 by
House of Anansi Press Inc.
110 Spadina Avenue, Suite 801
Toronto, ON, M5V 2K4
Tel. 416-363-4343
Fax 416-363-1017
www.anansi.ca

Distributed in Canada by
Publishers Group Canada
250A Carlton Street
Toronto, ON, M5A 2L1
Tel. 416-934-9900
Toll free order numbers:
Tel. 800-663-5714
Fax 800-565-3770

Distributed in the United States by
Independent Publishers Group
814 North Franklin Street
Chicago, IL 60610
Tel. 800-888-4741
Fax 312-337-5985

08 07 06 05 04   1 2 3 4 5

NATIONAL LIBRARY OF CANADA CATALOGUING IN PUBLICATION DATA

Daigle, France
[Petites difficultés d'existence. English]
Life's little difficulties / France Daigle ; translated from the
French by Robert Majzels.

Translation of: Petites difficultés d'existence.
ISBN 0-88784-700-5

I. Majzels, Robert, 1950– II. Title. III. Title: Petites difficultés
d'existence. English.

PS8557.A423P4713 2004   C843'.54   C2004-901132-4

Cover design: Matthew Wearn
Author photograph: Marc Xavier LeBlanc
Typesetting: Tannice Goddard

 Canada Council   Conseil des Arts
for the Arts   du Canada

ONTARIO ARTS COUNCIL
CONSEIL DES ARTS DE L'ONTARIO

*We acknowledge for their financial support of our publishing program the Canada Council
for the Arts, the Ontario Arts Council, and the Government of Canada through the Book
Publishing Industry Development Program (BPIDP). This book was made possible in part
through the Canada Council's Translation Grants Program.*

*The author wishes to thank the Canada Council for the Arts and the New Brunswick
Direction for the Arts for their financial support in the writing of this book. Thanks also
to Gérald Leblanc for his kind permission to reproduce excerpts from his collection*
Je n'en connais pas la fin, *published by Éditions Perce-Neige in 1999.*

Printed and bound in Canada

21.

SHI KE / GNAWING AND BITING THROUGH

AGAIN AND AGAIN, Carmen turns the note over in her hand. She can read the message backwards easily, the felt pen's ink having seeped through the paper. *I've decided to love you till the day I die.* She rereads the words the right way round, and remains annoyed by the wilfulness of the phrase. She puts the note back in her pocket without bothering to refold it. For the rest of the day, she will be unable to shake the idea that anyone could actually decide to love another person.

Terry has taken to consulting the Yi Jing during the day's quiet moments, between runs on the river. On a shelf in the pilothouse of the *Beausoleil-Broussard* — one of the tour boats thanks to which the Petitcodiac has almost gained a measure of affection — he's made room for his jar of marbles and his four books of interpretation, three in English and one in French. He's particularly fond of the French manual, a gift from Carmen, purchased in Paris.

    Terry likes to take his time consulting the oracle, reading each book's interpretation of the potential forces in play at the time of undertaking a particular divination.

Each book has its own tone and Terry likes to take all the nuances into account.

"Intellectuel: that's what you are."

"Me? Intellectuel?"

Zed sometimes tags along with Terry on the boat.

"Someone reads four books on the same subject, I'd say that makes him an intellectuel. Can't be otherwise. When it's an abstract subject, I mean."

Terry feels compelled to reflect on what his friend has said. "All depends on what you do with it, I'd say."

Zed fiddles with one of the decorative ropes on the boat. "Even if you do nothing with it, you can still be an intellectuel. It's in your head just the same, isn't it?"

Terry's not sure just where to begin his explanation. "Naw. An intellectuel has got to talk. He can't just think. Anyway, how else are folks going to tell who's one and who isn't?"

Zed studies the horizon for a moment before replying. "Far as I'm concerned, it's got nothing to do with talking."

That evening, Carmen couldn't resist the temptation to ask Jocelyne, or Josse as everyone calls her, for her opinion. Josse is a coworker and not a close friend — Carmen hasn't known her long — but she has a good head on her shoulders and she doesn't beat around the bush. Carmen found her smoking in the employees' ultimate refuge, the storeroom where they keep the damaged or ready-to-junk billiard equipment.

"Would you say it's possible to decide to love someone till the day you die?"

"?!?"

Carmen was afraid she'd ruined her workmate's cigarette break.

Josse exhaled a long puff. "Say again?"

Carmen wasn't sure whether being asked to repeat the question was a good or bad sign. "Do you think it's possible to actually *decide* to love someone till the day you die?"

Josse inhaled a bit more smoke, exhaled. "To *decide* to love?" She took the time to draw in and expel one more puff before replying, which as far as Carmen was concerned was answer enough. "I suppose it's something a person could decide. Though it wouldn't do to set your mind too hard on it."

". . ."

". . ."

"Far as I'm concerned, a person who goes and decides to love till the day they die, sure sounds like their mind's hard set."

And with a final exhalation, Josse concluded, "There's worse, I suppose. Some folks get so they're dead set."

Once he'd read the introductions to each of his books on the Yi Jing, Terry opted for the method of consultation using marbles. One of the texts — not, he noted, the French one — gave far more detailed explanations of the possible methods of divination than the other three. It was this particular introduction that convinced Terry that the Chinese coins with holes in the middle that Carmen had given him along with the book from Paris were not the most appropriate tools. Anyway, they were too big;

when he shook them in his hands, there just wasn't enough room for them to move around and for each coin to express its particular energy. The Yi Jing was supposed to indicate the Way, and Terry felt this lack of space blocked movement from the start. He therefore opted for marbles. This method, which required sixteen marbles of four different colours, had been the object of extensive scholarly commentary and offered a compromise between the ritual requiring fifty stalks of the yarrow plant (whatever that was) and a simpler and quicker method using only three ordinary pennies.

"So, if you don't mind, I'll do it with marbles," he said, using the English word.

Terry reached into his pocket for the Chinese coins, which he had strung on a thin leather strap. He slipped the necklace over his head and around his neck.

"This way I won't be forgetting you were the one who gave me the Yi Jing."

"Well, you already knew about it before."

"Sure, but not like I do now. It comes from you, believe me."

Carmen had allowed herself to be convinced, all the more so because she found Terry divinely beautiful with the black leather string around his neck and the Chinese coins scattered in the small tuft of his sparse chest hair.

Zed was in the habit of dropping by the café every day.

"Was walking along the tracks this afternoon. Saw the back of that building they're planning to tear down on Church."

It had been a long time since the young man sitting with Zed had encountered someone who'd just walked along a railroad track. For a second or two he was unable to maintain his usual indifference to what was being said around him.

"And?"

"Would make a good place for lofts."

"Would cost a fortune, you mean."

Zed was generally an accommodating sort, but some attitudes had a way of irritating him. "No, what I meant was it would make a good place for lofts . . ." Then, dropping a few coins on the table to pay for his coffee, he revised the tense of his verb. "Will make a good place for lofts."

Watching Zed leave the café, the other young man felt a twinge of satisfaction at having stung him.

On his way home, Zed retraced his steps along the railroad tracks, feeling even surer of himself. He decided, once and for all, not to let his enthusiasm go to waste.

Rather than helping, Josse had actually added confusion to what Carmen was feeling. Now Carmen finds herself obliged to look at Terry in a new light. When they first met, she found him cute and a little shy, almost innocent.

But lately it seems she is constantly discovering a new, or, at the very least, unexpected strength in him. And now this decision to love her . . . It's the idea of deciding that worries her. Can't he just love her? Hasn't he simply loved her all along? Loved her for herself? Regardless of anything else? What has any sort of decision got to do with it? And will this evening never end, for God's sake! Carmen checks the time. She wants to go home, to find herself quietly alone, to look at Terry and the baby asleep together on the sofa in the living room, which often happens when she works right up to closing time.

Terry is beginning to go round in circles. Everything's done, even the diapers are folded. Carmen insisted on cotton diapers, for the sake of the environment, and he went along with it, though he wasn't entirely convinced of the real benefits. As for the apartment, it's as neat as it can be, even if it still looks cluttered with all the baby's paraphernalia.

The child is sleeping peacefully. Terry, remote control in hand, runs through the channels once, then begins again, but nothing really catches his fancy. He turns off the television, gets up, goes to look out the window, scratches his back as best he can, returns to his seat, picks up his guitar, tries once more to find that impossible chord, thinking how odd it's so difficult, given that the rest of the tune is so simple.

That evening, stretched out on his bed, Zed imagines the rear section of the building — a covered loading dock — as a shelter for a small farmers' market, while the front, which faces the street, would be ideal for boutiques. That would leave the two upper floors for the lofts. There might not be quite enough parking space, but that's better than too much of it. Zed is sick of those huge outdoor parking lots that create gaping emptiness everywhere. It's about time, as far as he's concerned, to squeeze ourselves in a bit, to force people to get together, to talk to each other.

21. Gnawing and Biting Through. Persevere in spite of an obstruction between the jaws. The truth is concealed, to act with determination brings success. Try to see things differently, to re-imagine.

There were only a few days of work remaining at the Petitcodiac Park, so Terry brought the Yi Jing books home that afternoon. Having put aside the guitar, with that problem chord still out of reach, he consulted the oracle without any particular question in mind, seeking only an overall reading of the situation.

Only the first line of the hexagram was changing, all the others were at rest. The result was hexagram 35, *Progress*, conditional on breaking with fixed ideas — the idea of pleasure, for example — and on your vision of each partner's role in a relationship.

50.

DING / THE CAULDRON

"Zed wants to do what?"

"He's already begun."

It had been a dog's age since Terry and Carmen had had the time for a heart-to-heart.

Terry passed the salad. "He's trying to convince folks that's got money to spare."

"Who, for example?"

"Lionel Arsenault."

"Lionel Arsenault? And how's that going, then?"

"Well, he hasn't said oui, and he hasn't said non."

Carmen took a first bite of her steak. "Mmm."

". . ."

"Mm-mmm."

"Not too shabby, eh?" Terry knew how to cook a steak. "Sooo . . . What do you think?"

Carmen swallowed a mouthful, and a sip of wine. Even the wine tasted particularly good. She looked at the label on the bottle. "I'd forgotten this wine was so good." She started in on her baked potato smothered in butter and sour cream.

"He says it won't be all that expensive."

"Aren't those places awfully hard to heat? I wouldn't enjoy freezing."

Everything tasted great to Terry, too. And the baby tucked away and sleeping. A real feast! "And do you think I feel like freezing? Don't you find this place is starting to get a bit small? We've barely room to walk."

Carmen knew very well that Terry was right. She took another drink of wine. "Mmm. This wine is really fine!"

Terry accepted her sigh of contentment as a compliment. He congratulated himself secretly for inaugurating Carmen's three-day holiday with this special meal. He himself had not been working for a week. They had taken advantage of the situation to get a head start, to tidy up the apartment, and even to take afternoon naps before Carmen went to work.

"I doubt Lionel Arsenault'll be putting money in if there's none to make out of it."

"Anyways, Zed's pretty well convinced. He's close to convinced me as well."

"Appears that way."

"So you're going to do it?"

Sylvia, Lionel Arsenault's wife, knew her husband well. She knew that, if he was talking about a project, it was because he'd more or less made up his mind to go ahead.

"There's something about that fellow that pleases me. I'm curious to see just how far the thing might go."

Sylvia swallowed a bite of salmon. She never served anything but fish on Fridays. A superstition, really.

"Ever since you've taken to going down to Joe Moka's for a coffee, seems to me you're more . . . I mean, you're less . . ."

Lionel Arsenault laughed. "You mean those artists are starting to rub off on me?"

Was that the way art spread its influence? By splattering? By a gradual abrasion?

"Seems so."

He appeared more relaxed, too. Sylvia thought it had something to do with his getting older. But maybe it was true that, as one aged, art and life became one. She'd read something like that in a magazine.

"In any case, it would be a good thing if others could benefit from all that money."

Lionel Arsenault nodded, and swallowed a mouthful.

Zed was still living with his parents. That evening his uncle and aunt had joined the family for supper.

"Well then, Zed, what are you up to?"

It was perhaps a trick question, but this time Zed was ready.

"Matter of fact, I am working on something. Can't talk about it just yet."

Zed had only to open his mouth to revive the apparently unconditional admiration of his two younger sisters, who squirmed with pleasure on their chairs. On the other hand, as Zed had expected, his father added a note of skepticism to the general surprise and curiosity his answer had provoked.

"Zed thinks like an artist. It's not his fault, really."

The girls broke into a chorus of giggles. It was their way of rejoicing for Zed that things were not his fault. But a look of disapproval from their mother quickly recalled them to order.

"If it's a fault at all . . ." Aunt Annette did not approve of constantly putting young people on the hot seat. She took up her nephew's defence. "Some things take time; you can't force them."

There followed a few moments during which nothing could be heard other than the sounds produced by diners gathered around Acadian chicken soup.

"There's a whole lot more fricot . . . Georges . . . Annette . . . ?"

Zed finally broke the tension. "And what is it you've got planned for tonight? A game of cards?"

His mother's mood brightened immediately. "Now there's a fine idea! I wouldn't mind a game or two of Deux-Cents."

50. The Cauldron. Supreme good fortune. All is proceeding according to the natural order of things, just as wood is kindled by flames. A ritual, sacrificial meal is served in the home. Your interior life leads you to consider the material side of life in a relaxed manner. The second line, changing, yields hexagram 56, The Wanderer: one's constant travels come to an end when one finds a satisfactory place to live.

"We could just as well stay here a while longer, even if it is small. We're not so badly off, really. It's just that Zed seems so sure this thing'll work."

Carmen likes Zed well enough. And she's happy to see he and Terry are good friends.

"He doesn't want to talk it up too much. Wants to do it his way."

Something else is worrying Terry. "Another thing I wanted to tell you . . ."

Carmen likes this sort of suspense.

"The other day, I smoked a cigarette with him."

Carmen is doubly surprised. First, she and Terry quit smoking almost a year ago. And then: "Zed smokes? Since when?"

"Well, he doesn't, does he. Smoke, I mean. Only he found a pack with two cigs left in it. It was a kind of joke to smoke them."

Carmen takes a moment to digest the confession, then she imagines Terry and Zed — probably on board the boat — committing this misdemeanour. "Was it good, then?"

"Well, was and wasn't."

". . ."

". . ."

"Did it make you want to smoke more?"

Terry thinks a bit before replying. "Not really. Well, you know how it is . . ."

The fact that Carmen did not react badly reassures Terry. "C'est pas si bad, is it?"

In truth, Carmen finds the incident funny more than anything, but she doesn't want to let Terry off too lightly. "I suppose that's up to you to decide."

"You're not going out, then?" Zed's mother had opened the door a crack and spied Zed lying on his bed.

"I might go over to Doc's."

His mother found it odd that her son was still hanging

around at home at this hour. She worried that he'd been hurt by the talk at the supper table.

"Who's winning, then?"

"Annette's the only one who's picked up cards worth anything so far."

A brief silence ensued. His mother couldn't quite evaluate her son's state of mind.

"I don't know, feels like I'm still hungry."

Zed's mother was relieved. "There's some strawberry pâté left. Go fetch yourself some before your uncle gets his mitts on it."

Zed got up cheerfully. "Bonne idée."

Once again, his mother noted how incapable of rancour he was. There were times she would not have blamed him for harbouring some.

Terry didn't know what to say. "What? You think it sounds . . . intellectuel?"

Not that Carmen wanted to ruin their evening together, but this story about smoking a cigarette with Zed had got her thinking. It was time to clear up one or two things, she'd decided, and so she'd brought up the matter of his note that said he'd decided to love her till the day he died. Intellectual? She took a moment to consider this.

"Well, maybe so."

". . ."

"What is an intellectuel anyway?"

"Well, I'd say it's someone who thinks a whole lot, and who lets folks know it."

His reply was not much help to Carmen. "Name some, then, for example."

"I don't know . . . I suppose Hermé would be one."

". . ."

". . ."

"Would you say Pete Melanson was one?"

"Pete Melanson? Well, he'd like to be one, that's for certain."

". . ."

Terry got back to Carmen's original point. "I thought it was a fine note. Seemed nice to me, in my head, I mean, when I was writing it."

"In your head?"

And there it was, the very word he should not have used.

"Okay, okay, I get it." And, laughing, he concluded, "Next time, I'll buy roses."

That night Sylvia dreamed she was strolling along the boulevard Saint-Germain, wearing a panama hat and smoking a small cigar that left the scent of chocolate and spices in the air. It was as though she had just had sex with Pavarotti and had come away with love to spare. Passersby in the street stopped in their tracks, enthralled by the delicate blue wisp of smoke unravelling in the air above. The panama swayed gently down the avenue, in time with Sylvia's hips against her sleeping husband's thigh.

17. SUI / FOLLOWING

ZED TOOK ADVANTAGE of the real estate agent's being late to explain his strategy to Lionel Arsenault: "It's best we don't talk too much about what we're planning to do with it in front of him. That way, we give ourselves more of a chance to keep the price down."
They were walking around the somewhat dilapidated warehouse. The ground around them was littered with bits of wood and metal.
"At first, it was artists who got the idea to live in places like this. They were abandoned buildings, so they got them for next to nothing. Lots of times, was illegal even. Matter of fact, they were squatting. They needed room for their paintings and such things. Started in Berlin, then spread to New York. Seems the idea really comes from Paris, way back when artists lived in attics."
This information reinforced Lionel Arsenault's favourable impression of Zed.
"The plan would be just to make the building . . . like . . . functional. We wouldn't have to finish inside each loft. That would be up to chacun. Well, still, it means electricity, heating, replacing the windows."
"Plumbing."

"Plumbing."

The colours of the façade in front of which Zed and Lionel Arsenault had stopped formed bizarre patterns.

"Here they tore down an extension. This was the colour of the walls inside. Would be nice to keep some of it, it's comme beau."

Lionel Arsenault was trying to see the beauty Zed saw there.

"Other thing about lofts, we could — I mean we ought to, as much as possible — use old materials, odd things lying about. Abandoned. Well, not for everything. There again, all depends . . ."

". . ."

"Has to make sense now, doesn't it? We'll need a whole lot of ideas. Have to take the time to gather some up, talk to folks, carpenters, architects. Look around, see what's lying about. There's stuff we could get for a song."

A car drove up on the property. The real estate agent got out, walked toward the two men, extending a hand. "Sorry I'm late," he said, addressing them automatically in English.

In the afternoons, when Carmen was home, Terry liked to go downtown for a coffee. In truth, coffee alone would not have drawn him there, but it gave him a chance to meet with friends and catch up on the news.

That day Terry sat down at Lisa-Mélanie's table. "Well, if it isn't Lisa-M.! How's it going, then?"

Lisa-Mélanie, a music student some folks insisted on calling Lisa-Minnelli, even though she looked nothing like the original, liked Terry's way of shortening her name.

"Hi, Terry!"

They made small talk for a while, until Lisa-M. declared, "Lately, I don't know what's wrong . . . every time I brush my teeth, I feel like throwing up. Don't know if it's the toothpaste or what . . ."

Terry was not without his practical side. "Have you changed brands, then?"

"No."

Terry tried to imagine the situation. "So, you feel nauseous and all?"

Lisa-M. nodded. "I even have to be careful not to brush too far back."

". . ."

". . ."

"Could be the drain."

"The drain?"

"Lots of girls don't like that hole."

"Vraiment? First I ever heard of it."

Terry shrugged. He wasn't going to make a big deal of it. "How do you like university?"

Lisa-M. rocked her head first to one side, then the other. "I can't wait for Christmas. I'm going to Mexico with Pierre and Antoine. Pomme too, I hope. If he can scrape together the money. Pierre's uncle's got a condo in Puerto Vallarta. He'll be coming back here for Christmas, so he's lending his condo to Pierre."

It seemed a slightly incongruous quartet to Terry, but he chose not to dwell on it. It might be just an idea she was tossing around.

"And how's Carmen? It's been a dog's age since I saw her."

"Pas pire."

"She still working at Dooly's?"

"Uh-huh. She wouldn't mind if the manager left . . . so she could take his place."

"She's smart enough to do the job, too."

". . ."

"And what about Étienne? He's so cute."

"Well, he's got teeth now."

"Aw! Even cuter, I bet."

They chatted a while longer before Terry got up to go. In the end, he left without having been served and consequently without spending a penny. Which was all right by him, since every penny counted when he was unemployed.

Zed was happy to have something to tell his parents, at last.

"How serious is he, then?"

"He's ready to make an offer."

Zed's two little sisters listened, just waiting for a chance to laugh, but in vain.

"And what about you? What would you be doing?"

"Well, I'm the one'll be putting the whole thing together. Come up with ideas, materials, people to do the work. Folks to buy . . . or rent, we haven't decided yet."

This, the two girls figured, was a good enough excuse to burst into giggles. Which they did.

Zed's father, on the other hand, continued to express his doubts. "Well, you know the City'll never approve it, will they."

"I'm thinking we can convince them. I mean, it makes perfect sense."

His mother's eyes were full of admiration. "And when is it you begin, then?"

"He says I'm to be on the payroll as of Monday."

This was good news, but Zed's mother's curiosity was not entirely satisfied. "This coming Monday, or last Monday?"

Zed shrugged. "Either way . . ."

His father would not relent. "Two hundred and fifty dollars a week is not a whole lot of money."

"I figure it's fine. More than fine, really. Especially since I'll end up with a place to live."

Zed's mother felt a pang in her heart. She was afraid to discover that Zed might not be happy at home.

For her benefit, although he doubted it would suffice to reassure her, Zed added, "A place of my own, I mean."

Again his sisters exploded into giggles. Zed turned to face them. "Will you come to visit me, then?"

They replied in unison: "Ouiiii!"

17. Following. Inescapable, brings supreme success, great gain. Insight. The way is clear. Personal relations are very important: love, loyalty, open-mindedness, reciprocity, complicity. Better to abandon an unreasonable project if it is cause for conflict with loved ones. Taking care of someone necessarily leads to what must follow. A changing fifth line yields hexagram 51, Thunder. Courage, an unexpected upheaval initially provokes fear, then laughter and joy. Renewed energy, along with life and love.

Once he'd checked his figures, Pomme picked up the phone. "Lisa?"
"Hi, Pomme!"
"I'd say it's a go."
"You mean you're coming? Phew!"
"André finally came up with the money he owed me. So when do we buy the tickets?"
"Have you spoken to Pierre and Antoine, then?"
"No, not yet."
"All right, I'll give them a call. We could do it on Monday."
"Monday won't do. I'm supposed to work all day, if it doesn't rain. And they're not calling for rain."
"Well, we could buy yours just the same. What are you up to tonight?"
"Don't know yet. Zed's supposed to give me a call."
"We're all going to L'Osmose."
"Hmm . . . not sure I feel like it. Who's the DJ?"
"I think it's Bosse."
"Josse? Has she quit working at Dooly's, then?"
"Not Josse. Bosse."
"Oh, well. I guess I won't go, then."

Even though she hated to venture onto such treacherous terrain, Zed's mother couldn't help herself that evening, in the bedroom. "Seems to me you don't give him much of a chance."

". . ."

"Can't you see he's managing?"

Zed's father sighed. His wife wasn't wrong, but somehow he couldn't quite believe in his son's project. "They're dreamers."

"Lionel Arsenault a dreamer? Well, if that's the case, I'd say he hasn't done badly with his dreams."

Her husband having nothing to reply to that, she continued: "I don't want to bother you with it, but you know how you've always said your dad never encouraged his kids, how he was never there for you? Well, seems to me you're doing pretty much the same with Zed . . ." She hesitated between leaving it at that and going on, reopening an old wound. But she couldn't stop the words coming out. "I know he's not your birth child and that the two of you have your differences, but I thought things were going much better between you. It's hard for him as well, can't you see that?"

Her husband did not feel the strength, or perhaps the will, to defend himself.

"Anyhow, I think he's awfully clever to be doing this thing . . . and, seems to me, we ought to encourage him."

Though she thought she was done talking, she found herself adding, in a lighter tone, "It's kind of exciting really, the whole idea! I'm sure I'd be awfully proud if it worked."

Carmen felt the boss had been truly unfair with Josse. It made her angry to see him abuse his power like that. After all, it wasn't Josse's fault if her childhood friend had died.

"Asshole." Josse used the English expression.

"What did he say to you, then?"

"That I was taking too many days off."

Carmen thought as much. Although she'd noticed that Josse had been making an effort. "You've been a lot better lately."

"That's what I thought."

". . ."

"I don't care. I'm going pareil."

The funeral was the next evening.

Now as her shift came to an end, Josse couldn't untie her apron fast enough to get out of there. She turned her back to Carmen. "Can you get this damn thing undone, so's I can haul my ass out of here?"

Carmen did as she was asked. "I'll talk to him, try to explain."

"You do what you please, but if I lose my job on account of him, that won't be the end of it . . . le crisse!"

Later that evening, when things got a bit slow in the billiard hall, Carmen tried to talk to the manager. "I know it's none of my business really, but we could have got along without Josse tomorrow. Billy was ready to replace her."

"You're right. It is none of your business."

The man was exasperating, but Carmen kept trying all the same. "It's been a month she's hardly missed a day of work, and she's a good waitress. Seems to me . . ."

"There's some here think it's easy running a business. Well, Josse went too far, so I put my foot down. That's all there is to it."

"It's not her fault that fellow decided to die right now, is it? That's just the way it is."

"With Josse there's always something. Enough is enough."

Carmen was boiling inside. The manager's mind was as hard set as she'd feared. Dead set.

12.
PI / STAGNATION

"WHAT DO YOU say we skip Christmas?"

"Skip Christmas? Are you mad?" Carmen wasn't entirely awake yet; she was still working her way out of sleep.

"I mean, we ought to start our own Christmas, instead of going over to your folks', and then over to mine. Haven't we got our own family now?"

Carmen's only reply was to turn over toward Terry in the bed. It was an opening, and Terry took it.

"We might invite some folks over, cook a meal . . ."

Carmen was not averse to the idea. But, in practice, it seemed impossible. "It would kill my mom."

"I'm thinking your mom would understand, now we've got Étienne . . ."

"That's just it, isn't it. Now there's Étienne, I expect she'll want to see us that much more."

"We'd go pareil . . . even if it wasn't on Christmas Day."

To Carmen, this was starting to feel like a nightmare. "And on Étienne's first Christmas, can you imagine?!"

"All right, all right, then. Forget it. Was just an idea."

Zed is overwhelmed by the status he's been accorded in Lionel Arsenault's business. It's not just that he has a small office with a computer and telephone and all that, but, more importantly, the other employees treat him as an equal.

"Zed, let me explain how the lottery tickets work. I collect the money at the start of every month. No pressure, but everyone 'round here buys in, even Lionel. Costs ten dollars a month. Any small amount we win, we leave dans l'potte."

Zed appreciates the freedom to come and go as he pleases, because his project requires that he find inspiration in all sorts of places, talk to all kinds of people, hang about in locations one doesn't normally frequent.

"And what was it you were planning to do with those panels over there?"

"They're off to the dump. À cause? You want them, then?"

Zed had considered buying a small second-hand car to get around, but in the end he'd found an old truck, which came in handy.

"Back your truck in here."

Then: "You're saving us a trip to the dump . . . not to mention we've got to pay to throw things in there now."

And finally, inevitably: "That old building? Looks about ready to crumble!"

In the café:

"I've found a name for Zed's project . . ."

Terry wasn't particularly fond of talking to this slightly sinister fellow who had a way of denigrating everyone, but one couldn't always avoid him.

"Should be called 'Loft in Space.'"

Although the pun was funny, Terry knew the guy was really laughing at Zed, calling him a dreamer and his project a delusion.

"I don't think he wants a name en anglais."

"Don't tell me Zed's into that whole can of worms as well."

"I mean to say I don't think he'd like a name that works only en anglais."

"Well then, isn't the word 'loft' anglais?"

Terry shrugged. He had no defence for such an argument.

". . ."

"Anyway, there'll probably just be French folks living there. Maybe a couple of anglais mixed in. Like at Aberdeen."

The fellow agreed, but he wasn't done yet. "I tell you, I've just about had my fill of this anglais-français thing. It's depressing. A fellow's always got to be on one side or the other."

Terry shrugged again. "That's the way it is. Not much we can do about it." He turned away, to let the other man know he had no desire to continue the conversation.

"Pareil, I say it's too much."

The firing of Josse, who, in the end, called in sick in order to attend her friend's funeral, caused a stir. As soon as they heard about her firing, the billiard hall employees all put on their coats and walked out. Carmen was proud of their solidarity.

"I never knew we were so close as that. Everyone's got their own life, I suppose. It took something that just didn't make sense to bring us together. It's times like this you see that folks have got their hearts in the right place after all."

The manager not only reversed his decision, he agreed to set up a committee to look into establishing fair and equal working conditions for all employees. But Carmen was looking beyond that.

"He had no choice but to back down; he won't be around much longer."

She began to clear the way more actively to taking his place. "No one ought to have to work two weekends in a row. And we ought to organize stuff for young people and old folks."

"Old folks?"

"And why not? Most afternoons the place is empty."

"And what would you do with young folks, then?"

"Don't know exactly, do I, but someone told me billiards could be good for a math class, 'cause of the angles and all."

There were two sealed envelopes on Zed's desk. He opened one. It was his first paycheque. When he opened the other, he thought there'd been a mistake. He found the administrative secretary and showed her the two cheques.

"I don't get it. One of them must be my pay, but the other . . ."

"Monsieur Arsenault told us to do that. I thought you knew à cause."

Zed shrugged. Nor did he understand why the employees sometimes referred to Lionel Arsenault by his given name and sometimes as Monsieur Arsenault.

"Well, go and ask him, why don't you? He's in today."

Zed made his way over to Lionel Arsenault's office, knocking gently on the frame of the door, which was ajar.

"Zed! Come on in! How are things?"

"Fine! Fine!" Zed was surprised by his own enthusiasm. It was as though the boss's confidence was contagious. He also wanted to be quick about it — so as not to take up too much of the businessman's time — but Monsieur Arsenault seemed to want to chat.

"Well then? How're things coming along?"

"It's coming along. I'm starting to put some of the pieces together. I'll have more to show you in a week or two."

"No problem. I trust you."

Zed showed him the two cheques.

"Your first pay?"

"Oui, but . . ."

"Let's say the other one's a gift from my wife."

Zed was totally in the dark.

"You bought a truck, didn't you?"

"Oui, but . . ."

"How much did it cost you?"

Zed was a little embarrassed. He wasn't sure he'd made a good deal, car mechanics not being his strength. He was afraid Lionel Arsenault would realize it and judge him less competent. "Two thousand, seven hundred. I think that's reasonable. I was in a hurry, kind of . . ."

Lionel Arsenault shrugged. "Don't ask me, I don't know

a thing about that stuff. My wife's the one buys the cars in our family."

Zed was relieved.

Lionel Arsenault continued, "My wife — Sylvia — knows your Aunt Annette very well."

"Really?"

"They were talking about you the other day. So the other cheque is for the truck."

Zed wasn't sure what to think. "I was figuring to pay for it moi-même. I mean, I wouldn't ask you."

"I know. And you didn't ask, did you. But you know my wife, when she's got it in her head to do something . . . Anyway, it's only fair." Lionel Arsenault waited a few seconds, long enough for Zed to get past his embarrassment. "Was there anything else, then?"

"No, no . . . And, well, like I said, I'll have more to show you by the end of next week."

"No problem."

Zed took his leave, but Lionel Arsenault called him back as he was walking out the door. "I saw the mayor day before yesterday. Talked to him about our project. He wanted to hear more. I told him you'd go round to see him. We'll be needing him, I figure, at some point."

It was then that Zed realized just how much confidence Lionel Arsenault had in him. "No problem!"

As Zed passed the secretary's desk, she asked him if he'd worked everything out.

Zed had to stop and ask: "Is he always so nice?"

The secretary laughed. It was all Zed needed to hear. Back at his desk, he took a moment to celebrate in secret.

The better Zed got to know him, the higher Lionel Arsenault rose in his esteem, and his wife Sylvia wasn't far behind.

12. Stagnation. It is hazardous to struggle against people with petty motives, to resist them only confuses the situation. It furthers one to withdraw, to avoid taking on responsibilities. Create a peaceful haven. Obstacles will dissolve of themselves if you give yourself a clear objective. A changing fifth line yields hexagram 8, Union. Change is everywhere. Find allies or a protector, join a group, become its leader. You will find joy by allowing yourself to follow the way of harmony and pleasure. Do not hesitate to consult the oracle again, for it has more to tell you.

Before they got down to work, Zed gave Terry a tour of the building. The young men didn't talk much: the site spoke for itself. They ended up simply standing in the midst of the space.

"Gee . . . It really feels like it starts in your heart and goes up. It's like being . . . entranced . . . envoûté."

Even though he came often now, Zed always fell under the spell of the place.

"First time I use that word, by the way . . ."

"Good word."

Zed glanced at his watch. "I don't have much time . . ."

The two friends moved outside to unload the truck.

"And what is it you're planning to do with all this?"

"Not sure yet. I'm thinking they might make nice walls. In the hallways or something."

"The covers, or the vinyls themselves?"

"Don't know yet. Either one, or both. Ça dépend." Zed pulled several sleeves from one of the boxes. "See, we could make a montage of colours. Maybe we'll put the sleeves on one wall and the records on the wall opposite . . ."

Terry looked into the truck. There had to be thousands. "Where did you get them all?"

"I bought everything they had at Cindy's, and the rest in a couple of other places. Cost almost nothing." Zed picked up a particularly ugly cover. "I guess there's some we won't be using."

The two young men began transporting the cases of old records into the building.

"Funny we call them vinyls now. Before they were just records."

Zed thought for a moment before replying. "I knew you were an intellectuel."

On his way home from work that evening, Lionel Arsenault picked up the Chinese takeout his wife had ordered for supper. He did so happily; he liked to feel that his wife could rely on him, even for the little things.

At home, they set the table together and sat down to eat.

"Zed got the cheque for his truck today."

"And?"

"Big surprise. Didn't quite know what to say. By God, that boy makes me laugh."

"I wouldn't mind meeting him one of these days. Annette says he's like a son to her. She was all set to adopt him if Dorine hadn't been able to keep him."

The Chinese food was especially delicious.

"How old was Dorine then?"

"Don't know . . . twenty-two, maybe twenty-three."

"So, not so young."

"It was an awful shame just the same."

". . ."

". . ."

"Does he know his real father?"

"I don't know. I don't think so."

Lionel Arsenault dropped the last shrimp shell onto his plate and wiped his fingers. "Just the same, that boy'll go far. He's got it in him."

Terry was surprised to hear a knock at the door at such a late hour. "Zed?"

"I was thinking I'd talk to you this morning. Just didn't have the time."

"Come on in! Rentre! Great. Someone to share a drink. I was just starting to get bored."

"Must be a drag, Carmen working late so many evenings."

"I try not to complain . . ." Terry brought two beers from the kitchen. "Well. So what's up?"

Zed tipped his bottle and drank before answering. "First off, what's up is Lionel Arsenault's truly amazing."

"Well, I pretty much figured that."

"No. I mean, the man's totally all right."

". . ."

"The more I get to know him, the more I find I want to address him as vous."

". . ."

Zed took another drink of beer. "Second thing is, I'm sure this thing of ours is going to work. Absolument sûr."

". . ."

"Third of all . . . I'd like you to come and work with me."

"!!!"

"And in time, I'm pretty sure, there'll be work for Carmen, too."

"Gee! Keep talking! There's plenty of beer in the fridge!"

16.

YU / ENTHUSIASM

"He's thinking of a small bar downstairs. Something tranquille, good music, a couple of pool tables. Sofas. You know, something comfortable. More like a lounge." Terry had not been able to sleep. He'd sat up waiting for Carmen.

"Yes, well, it takes money to start a thing like that, doesn't it? And what happens if it goes belly up? It takes a whole lot of folks to keep a bar going, believe me!"

Terry was not about to contradict her.

"At least at Dooly's I won't lose my shirt if things go wrong."

Terry had to admit that Carmen might be right. But he couldn't help feeling that Zed's project wasn't crazy either. "Well, suppose I went along and worked with him, for a start I mean? Just to help out. We could see how things go. He's got loads of good ideas."

"I suppose."

Terry could feel Carmen was holding something back. "Something's bothering you, for sure."

Carmen did not deny it. "It's just that I can't imagine us living there with the kid. Seems to me it's no place for a child . . . not to mention two."

Terry wasn't sure he'd understood. He looked Carmen

squarely in the eyes. "Are you saying what I think you're saying?"

Carmen blushed a bit, lowered her eyes. "I'm not certain yet, but it sure feels like it."

"Pregnant? You're pregnant? We're pregnant?" Terry took Carmen in his arms. He wouldn't have been able to say why, but the prospect of another child overjoyed him. "C'est great! C'est just great!"

Carmen relaxed in Terry's embrace. "I don't know if I'm tired or what . . . Seems like there's too much happening."

Terry caressed her hair. "Don't you worry, Belle! Just worry pas, everything's going to turn out fine! You'll see."

As she did every Saturday morning, Sylvia Arsenault — maiden name Gaudet — went down to the farmers' market to do some shopping. She'd tanked up her car in Shediac before heading to Moncton.

"Well, Mélanie! How are things with you, then?"

In her hometown of Shediac, Lisa-Mélanie was known simply as Mélanie.

"How's university?"

"I guess I like it . . ."

Sylvia sensed something not quite right, but she did not pursue it. "I didn't know you were still working here."

Throughout her adolescence, Lisa-Mélanie had toiled loyally in her parents' combination general store and gas station. "Oh, it's just to make a bit of extra money. I'm going to Mexico at Christmas."

"Mexico! Wow! And who with?" Sylvia knew Lisa-

Mélanie's mother well enough to imagine the fuss the daughter's plan must have provoked.

"Three guys. Well . . . two of them are gay. And the other one, really, nobody knows. Could be he's nothing. Sexually, I mean."

The portrait made Sylvia laugh.

Lisa-Mélanie had always felt at ease with Sylvia, who was a lot more open than her own mother, even though the two women were the same age.

"And what does your mother say about it?"

"She's trying hard not to mind, but I know she minds just the same."

In spite of everything that was happening, Terry had slept well. Now, feeling the twinge of hunger, he decided not to wait for Carmen; he installed Étienne in the high chair and set to work in the kitchen. He also decided to shower Étienne with attention, in the hope that the boy would not mind playing by himself later, while Terry consulted the Yi Jing. He hadn't had the time to do so since the oracle had invited him to ask additional questions.

"A slice of ham for Étienne, a slice of ham for Dad. Two big eggs for Étienne, two big eggs for Dad. A bagel for Étienne, a bagel for Dad. And will you be wanting some smoked salmon on your bagel, Étienne?"

Étienne, listening to the outpouring of words, heard only cheerfulness.

"An espresso for Étienne, a cappuccino for Dad. Salt and pepper for Étienne, marmalade for Dad. Mmm . . . won't this be good!"

Étienne let his rattle drop to the floor. Terry picked it up, while keeping an eye on the eggs sizzling in the pan. He continued, "One rattle sunny side up, s'il vous plaît!" And he replied to himself, "Coming right up!"

Most Saturdays, by the time Lionel Arsenault got up, Sylvia was already out doing errands. He'd settle down with his coffee before the magnificent view of Shediac Bay and leaf through the newspapers he hadn't had time to read during the week.

That morning, it occurred to Lionel Arsenault that his wife might have a lover. He did not break off reading. It was just a passing thought, after all. Or a sexual fantasy. Which might explain . . . He took another sip of coffee. Maybe she was with him at that very moment. Lionel cleared his throat. No, it had to be a fantasy; he flipped over the page of the newspaper, continued reading.

Étienne was babbling away in his playpen.

16. Enthusiasm. Take pleasure in seeing things as they are, in serving others. Accumulated energy enables you to react fully and spontaneously. You hear the music of the spheres. Abandon your false contentment and take action. Give yourself the means to achieve your goals. Have confidence in your friends. Fraternity is the key to success.

Étienne was babbling more loudly now. *A changing line in the fourth position yields hexagram 2, Double Yin, resonance and receptivity.*

The earth has the power to nourish and give shape to all

things. Do not take the initiative, accept a role of support. Accomplish things as they present themselves, without concern. This could be the beginning of a new era, which will bring supreme success.

Étienne had ceased babbling and begun to scream. Terry got up, checked the baby's diaper, and set about changing it.

"Is this what you want? Eh, mon petit Étienne, is this the way you want it? Well, then, this is what you'll get! One thing at a time. What do you think of that, then? One diaper at a time. Eh? Hellooo?! Is there anybody home in there? Eh? Yoohoo? Hellooo?"

Étienne had no idea what it all meant, but the punctuation made him laugh.

And so what if she had a lover? As he turned another page of his newspaper, Lionel Arsenault thought that, if it was true, he would rather not know. It would only make him suffer. Because he could simply not imagine them separating. She was everything to him. In a manner of speaking.

Lionel Arsenault glanced at his watch as his eye roamed over the financial pages of the *New York Times* that he'd brought home in his luggage. He gleaned bits of information here and there as he sipped his coffee. His mind drifted back to the passion of the past night, the latest of many. Where had their renewed energy and abundance come from? As he turned the page, he noticed a small ad that seemed out of place: "The painter Étienne Zablonski and his wife Ludmilla wish to thank . . ."

He heard a car in the driveway. It was her. Lionel Arsenault watched Sylvia emerge from the car. She was more beautiful than ever. He could hardly believe it. He was completely besotted.

13.

TONG REN / FELLOWSHIP

THE ORACLE COULD not have been clearer. Terry had therefore followed through, efficiently and discreetly carrying out the first task Zed had assigned to him.

"Incroyable! Where did you get these?"

Terry was proud of his find, but he didn't want to show off. "It started with la compagnie Peters Combination Lock. They made all sorts of metal doodads, door handles, and metal sheets with flowery patterns for use in construction — was all the rage back then. Anyway, that company lasted all of five years. The folks that took over mostly made underwear up until the mid-fifties."

Zed glanced quickly at each photo before moving on.

"Hundreds of Acadiens worked in there making clothing. Truth is they pretty much lived in there. Made their meals and everything." Terry pointed to one of the photos. "Here you get a good view of the cafeteria."

"I thought there were no pictures of the inside of the building . . ."

Terry shrugged, as if to say: Just goes to show you can't believe everything you hear.

"I'm meeting an architect tomorrow, or day after tomorrow. Can I keep them?"

Terry handed Zed a file containing copies of the photographs and documents describing the building's history. "I made two sets like this. Figured we could use them."
Zed was impressed with Terry's organizational skills. "That's it, then . . . unless there's something else you'd like me to do?"
"Well, I suppose we ought to start figuring out how we're going to finance this whole affair."
". . ."
". . ."
The two young men walked toward Zed's truck.
"Could be something like a co-op might work."
"I leave it to you. You work it out."

13. Fellowship. The mechanism is well oiled, the gears smooth and silent. A great project will enlist many people and create harmony. New social structures must be invented that are balanced with clear objectives. A creative force moves toward the centre. A changing first line means there is no mistake, persevere! A changing line in the fifth place means a clear and loving voice smoothes over disarray within the group and brings joy once again. The two changing lines yield hexagram 56, The Wanderer —again! The voyage, life in exile or outside conventional social norms, is, in truth, a quest, a search for the fuel required to pursue one's existence. Identity is no longer fixed to a place of residence but rather to a calling to which one must respond.

Although Carmen had known the manager would end up going, she had not expected it to happen so quickly. "If they give me the job, I'll end up working like a madwoman through Christmas, won't I?"

". . ."

"And suppose it turns out I'm pregnant and I'm nauseous like last time . . ."

". . ."

"I'd rather they didn't know I'm pregnant."

". . ."

"So as not to muddle things up."

". . ."

"Things are muddled enough as it is."

". . ."

"Well? And what do you think?"

Terry was studying his and Carmen's relationship closely, because hexagram 13 had also suggested an archetypal couple relationship.

"Are you listening to me at all?"

"Pour sûr. I'm thinking about it."

"Oh, and here I thought you were snoozing."

". . ."

". . ."

"I wouldn't mind a book by Jung. For Christmas, I mean."

Carmen had heard the name before.

"I suppose I could just as well take one out of the library. Wouldn't do Étienne any harm to start going there." Normally he would have expected Carmen to react. She was very gung-ho on books for the child. Terry turned toward her. She was already fast asleep.

The famous Étienne Zablonski and his wife Ludmilla had put a small ad in the *New York Times* to inform their friends and acquaintances of the fire that had completely destroyed their Baltimore home. To astute readers, the message subtly thanked the pyromaniac who had lit the blaze. In fact, Étienne Zablonski had taken one of his paintings back from a Chicago gallery and sent it to the felon in gratitude. The painting was valued at close to ten thousand dollars, and Zablonski figured that in the event the pyromaniac did not like it — a distinct possibility — he could easily sell it after his release from prison, for example, when he would certainly require a bit of money.

For Zablonski and his wife, the fire had provided the impetus they needed to leave Baltimore and move to New York. The *New York Times* personal ads editor had to check that the ad in question did not contravene any law or moral code. The editorial board of the major daily, considering Zablonski's reputation and the elegant style of his message, decided to turn a blind eye to the unusual content of the missive, and bank on the likelihood that it marked an important crossroads in the painter's artistic career.

Zed hoped to attract a young architect who had nothing to lose and much to gain by participating in the project. "I thought of you because we don't want anything too nice looking."

The young architect thought it best to bide his time before deciding on the true significance of this opening remark.

Zed showed him photographs of luxurious lofts he'd cut out of magazines. "See, this for example . . . it's trop beau. Too fixed up. Too new."

"You're looking for something hard?"

Zed liked the concept. "C'est ça. I don't mean extreme hard, but hard, yes, I like that."

They talked for an hour, going through the file Terry had prepared. In the end, one small point remained unclear to the architect.

"And would I be getting paid, then? I didn't quite get whether or not you had any money."

Zed thought it best to be clear from the start. "Moitié-moitié. We've got money, sure, but it's not your usual money. We'll be a bit on the hard side there as well."

The architect put this reply aside with the earlier remark for later consideration. "And when could I have a look at the building?"

The prison authorities made an exception and allowed the pyromaniac to keep the painting in the cell he shared with three other criminals. The painting, a wild mix of colours and broken brush strokes, measured roughly two metres wide by one metre high. It practically filled the entire wall above the pyromaniac's upper bunk. At first, the other inmates in the cell made fun of the work, but gradually they began to refer to it with respect.

The three carpenters and the contractor Zed had led on a tour of the building stood for a moment in the parking lot to study the exterior. Zed had left them to go to a dealer in secondhand industrial goods in Amherst.

One of the carpenters lifted his cap and scratched the back of his neck. "I don't know . . . you mix new and old, it can get a bit tricky. Not as easy at it looks, no sir."

One of the other carpenters chewed slowly on his gum and said nothing.

"Going to take some imagination, c'est certain."

The third carpenter lit a cigarette, inhaled, appeared to forget the smoke — which finally came out through his nose — and let his gaze wander to a car honking in the street. He turned once more to look at the building.

The contractor, hands on hips, was also looking at the building.

The carpenter who had spoken continued: "Anyway, there'd be work all winter."

"That's for sure."

"Maybe more."

"Maybe more." The third carpenter was the type who crushed his cigarette butts meticulously under the tip of his boot.

The contractor, on the other hand, preferred to take the time to think before committing himself.

In the street, the same car passed in the opposite direction and honked again. This time, the three carpenters watched it go by.

One day, having nothing better to do, the four inmates decided to take down the painting, just to see what effect the bare wall would have on them. They were immediately struck — and moved, without truly realizing the effect was emotional — by the intimate relationship they had developed with Zablonski's work. They were troubled also by the bare wall, because they could not help but look on it as though it were a painting, which they were naturally drawn to interpret. Where in the past they had seen nothing, it was now impossible not to see something. They were shaken by this experience of surface, this sense of a total work, like an eggshell viewed from the interior. Their discovery of the very thickness of art — which was in fact only the reflection of their own abyss — almost drove them mad. In order to break what was a kind of spell, they set to work on the walls of the cell — in other words, on themselves — until they managed to sweat some meaning out of all these intersecting realities.

The three carpenters and the contractor had never worked together before and hardly knew each other. As a result, standing in the yard of the building to be transformed, they had little to say to one another; and yet, they seemed unable to take their leave.

At last, one of them spoke. "I'm thinking whether I know someone who'd like to live in a place like this . . ."

"Not my wife, en tout cas. Mind you, I might consider it . . . what with those big windows."

". . ."

"They'll have to find a way to get rid of the pigeons."

". . ."

Finally, the third carpenter took the plunge. "I like the idea, I do. Gives a fellow something different to work on. And I like the way they want to do it. There's enough good rubbish around, a real shame sometimes the stuff folks throw away, what's left to rot in the road."

The two other carpenters agreed.

After a moment of silence, one of the carpenters admitted, "Would you believe it, I've never worked in brick."

The others were stunned.

"And where do you come from, then?"

"Barachois. Grand-Barachois they call it now."

"Who is it decided that anyhow, I'd like to know."

The other man shrugged. He couldn't say.

"Sounds all right just the same, Grand-Barachois."

"Sure does make it sound bigger."

Just the same, the original surprise remained.

"Not even a fireplace?"

"Not even a fireplace."

". . ."

"Not that it bothers me, mind you."

30.

LI / THE CLINGING, FIRE

HARD TO BELIEVE, but it was all coming together without a hitch: the City had immediately come on board, the architect was hard at work, and preparations were underway to start construction the day after New Year's. Truly there was cause for celebration. All that remained was to come up with an official name for the project.
"And why not 'Loftstore' then?"
"In English?"
"Well, don't the French say 'Drugstore'?"
"The French have lost their language, if you ask me."
"'Round here, people'll say it in English anyhow, not in French."
"Sounds too much like 'Loft Story.'"
"I like 'Warehouse,' the way my granny used to say it: waar-a-oose."
"I don't want to burst your bubble, but that way of saying it most likely died with her."
"Well, she's not dead, is she. Just doesn't talk any more."
"There you go, then."
"And why not 'Aloft,' like 'lofty'? I mean, it's all up on high, isn't it? On account of the windows."
"Too sophistiqué."

"'Loftage'?"
". . ."
"'Lifticks'!"
"That doesn't mean anything, now does it?"
"'Liftage'?"
"And why not 'Liftosis,' if you're wanting something sick sounding."
"Dying, you mean."
". . ."
"And who is it ever said brainstorming was such a bright idea?"

Pomme had explained to Lisa-Mélanie why he'd given up on the Mexico trip.
"If you decide not to go, on account of I'm not going, I'll pay for your ticket, I will. If they won't refund it, I mean."
"Well, look who's rolling in dough."
"Never you mind. I said I'd pay for it, and I will."
". . ."
". . ."
"Will someone tell me what's going on 'round here this Christmas? It's like everyone's gone stark raving."
Pomme burst out laughing. "Don't I know it. C'est great!"

Carmen barely took the time to put down her bags.
"Which book by Jung was it you wanted? Must have been half a dozen over there."
"Is that right? Well, c'est pas grave. I don't have all that

much time for reading these days. Anyhow, there's no rush, really. I guess I figured it out on my own."

Now that she knew who Jung was, Carmen's curiosity was piqued. "And what is it you figured out, exactly?"

Terry came over and planted a kiss on Carmen's cheek. "I understand just how dependent I am on you."

"You, dependent on me? You do whatever you please!"

Terry thought for a moment before replying. "Still, ça change pas le fait, I'm dependent on you."

". . ."

". . ."

"Well, if you're so dependent, how is it you never do as I ask?"

"And what do you mean by that?"

"I mean, in the end, you always do what you please, don't you. Doesn't matter one bit what I think."

Terry had no idea where Carmen was going with this line of argument. "Such as?"

"Such as the loft."

"???"

"The way you're going on, you'd think it was decided we were moving in there."

"I'm only helping Zed. Being en chômage, I don't have much else to do, now do I? Anyway, I did tell him you weren't exactly thrilled about the idea."

"There you are! It's always my fault. Why is it you can't be on my side once in a while?"

The discussion seemed to be heading in a direction Terry was finding difficult to follow. Luckily, Étienne was spending the day with his grandparents.

67

"Well tell me then, how I am supposed to agree si j'agree pas?"

". . ."

"You want our kids to eat right out of the ground. Well, all right. I can see that. I just think we can fix it so they eat fresh grub even if we're living in a loft."

"What I said was they ought to be able to play outdoors, in a field or some such place, without us always having to be watching out for them."

As a matter of fact, Terry had raised this problem with Zed. "Zed thinks there'll be room enough for a park."

Carmen was suddenly furious. "Zed thinks! Zed thinks! Seems like that's all I ever hear 'round here any more: Zed thinks!"

Terry should have known this was no time to bring Zed into it, but now that the damage was done, he decided to have it out once and for all.

"And what's wrong with Zed tout d'un coup? Just last week, you were going on about how clever he was to think of all that, having Christmas over there . . ."

Carmen couldn't stand it. She burst into tears and fled into their room.

Terry followed her in and stretched out on the bed beside her. Gently he caressed her hair and let her cry.

"Don't you worry now, Belle. You know how it is being preggers and all. It'll pass. We'll do what's best for everyone. You go on and bawl your eyes out, and just worry pas."

Étienne and Ludmilla Zablonski tried to like New York. They visited art galleries and museums, but it seemed futile and superficial. And they emerged with little more enthusiasm from the miserable neighbourhoods they had hoped would be, at least, more authentic.

And yet, everything was going so smoothly. It was as though the search for a place had replaced the place itself. But where would it end? It was this unspoken question that Ludmilla expressed when she exclaimed, "What do you think will become of us?"

Étienne Zablonski was familiar with this sort of abandon. He had learned long ago to appreciate these moments empty of any future.

"Let's go to Canada!"

"Canada?"

"Yes. It will be winter there now. The snow. The cold. Blizzards."

"Brrrr . . ."

Once more, Étienne Zablonski told his wife of his meeting with the young couple, Terry and Carmen, in France, the year before. Strangely, it was as though he were telling the story for the first time, and, equally strange, it was as though Ludmilla, too, were hearing it for the first time.

"And they spoke French?"

"Yes, yes. They're Acadians."

Ludmilla Zablonski seemed to remember something from long ago. "Oh yes, the Acadians. I saw something on TV about them. They're very short, aren't they?"

"Short?" Étienne Zablonski tried to remember if Terry and Carmen were short. "No, I don't think so. Well, I'm not sure."

". . ."

"..."

"Well, let's go to Monk-town and find out."

Carmen had almost stopped crying. Terry was still by her side.

"You ought to call in sick. You could sleep a bit. I'll make us un bon souper. My mom can take Étienne for the night, she won't mind a bit. We can talk it through, if you like."

Carmen said nothing, but she seemed to have calmed down somewhat.

"I can call, if you like."

Carmen sniffed; a moment passed.

"Well, how about it? Shall I call, then?"

Carmen sniffed again. Terry had the feeling she was trying to get closer to him as she shifted her position. He planted a kiss on her head, stretched out his arm, and picked up the telephone receiver. He dialled the number. As Carmen did nothing to stop him, he continued. "Josse? How are you, then?"

"Could be better. Everyone's sick. I'm almost on my own over here."

Terry screwed up his courage. "Justement, Carmen doesn't feel well non plus. She won't be coming in to work tonight. Looks to me like the flu."

"She did look pale yesterday! Oh well, we'll manage. You take good care of her, mind you. That woman saved my life, she did."

"Mine too."

Terry hung up. Carmen twisted around in the bed, wrapped her arms around Terry, and hugged him tight.

When he heard his father — or at least the man he'd called his father since the age of six — preparing to leave by the side door, Zed got up from the dinner table and went to find him.

"I'll back my truck out."

"Give me the keys, I'll do it."

"No, no, I'll go. I shouldn't have put it there, should I."

"No bother. I'll do it."

Zed dropped his keys in the palm of the outstretched hand. "All right then, if you like . . ." He returned to the table, sat down, and continued to eat in silence.

The side door opened again.

"Zed, I'm putting your keys here . . . Your truck's not all that aisé to start. I'd say it was your plugs. I'll take a look at it samedi, if you like."

Zed was surprised by his father's kindness. True, he'd seemed more relaxed lately.

"Sure! If you don't mind . . ."

The older man left. Zed stole a glance at his mother, who had continued to eat, but he did not catch her eye.

With dessert, his mother gave him the cue. "And what are you up to tonight, Zed?" The two had agreed in advance on the scenario they would follow.

"I've got a big evening. We're decorating the Christmas trees over at the lofts. And we've still beaucoup de decorations to put up as well." He turned to his two sisters. "How would you like to come along and give us a hand?"

Clearly excited by the prospect of Zed's invitation, the two girls turned quickly to their mother to gauge the proposal's chance of success.

"Have you got homework?"

"I'm almost done."

"Me too!"

Zed checked his watch. "Would a half hour be enough time, then?"

The girls jumped for joy, and scurried off to their room.

"Dad's been de bonne humeur lately . . . Is there something up?"

"Someone gave him a bit of a talking to. I suppose it did him good."

Zed did not understand. "Someone talked to him?"

"Oui. I did."

Now Zed thought he understood. He continued to clear the table, wondering if he ought to ask the next question.

"And does that mean you'll be coming at Christmas?"

"I'd say we're all coming, yes."

Zed felt a sudden tightening in his stomach and his face growing red.

His mom knew her son well. She turned to him, put her hands on his shoulders, and looked him squarely in the eyes. "Anyhow, I'm coming and that's for sure."

Zed knew his mother loved him, but the determination she was showing on his behalf at this moment in his life made him feel like crying. And that's exactly what he did, in the arms of his mother, who cried right along with him, because she understood all too well. The jag lasted only a minute, maybe two. It could have lasted longer, but crying over two lives would have taken too long, so they pulled themselves together, burst out laughing, and finished clearing the table.

Terry had proceeded methodically. He'd spoken to his mother, who had read between the lines that the young couple needed an evening together, and he'd prepared everything for their supper without cooking anything, because he hadn't wanted to wake Carmen, who clearly needed to rest. He even had time now to read his Yi Jing. Once more he was bowled over by the accuracy of the oracle.

30. The Clinging, Fire. The light will shine brightly if the idea is presented gently and clearly.

Four changing lines out of six was a lot. The first called on him to recognize his own errors. The second spoke of a flash in the pan, a minor incident of little importance in his life. The third, of a flood of tears that opened the way and allowed a relationship to go forward. And the fourth, of perfection and abundance accorded to those who learn to adhere rigorously to what's essential. However, these changing lines yielded hexagram 39, *Obstruction*. Terry was relieved to find that this hexagram was not as disturbing as its name implied. It seemed that the problem of the couple did not require compromise to be resolved. They need only forget it for harmony to return. *Remain yourself and turn to the southwest, for a fresh wind will blow from there.*

"Hmm!"

This mention of the southwest surprised Terry. He wondered if he should take it literally or in some metaphorical sense.

The telephone rang.

"Terry? Zed. Shall I pick you up?"

"No. I won't be coming de soir. Carmen's trop fatiguée to go to work, so I'll be staying home with her. It'll do us good."

Zed was glad to see how Terry took care of Carmen.

"Pas de problème. Enjoy yourselves! We'll talk tomorrow."

As he hung up, Terry looked up to find Carmen standing in the living room doorway. She did not look entirely awake yet.

"What time is it, anyhow?"

"Seven-thirty."

". . ."

"Étienne's going to sleep over at my mom's."

". . ."

"Are you hungry, then?"

"I'm famished."

"Do you really want to put lights in all the windows? On both sides, I mean?"

"And why not, pray tell? It'll be nice for the folks who go by on the train."

Zed bowed to Pomme's decision. Pomme had gladly taken charge of decorating the warehouse for the big bash they had planned. Zed climbed down from the stepladder, plugged in one more string of electric candles to the others, pushed the ladder over a couple of metres, climbed back up, and attached the lights exactly as Pomme wanted them.

Pomme, meanwhile, was raising the fifth tree. He figured they needed six of them, well spaced out, to properly fill the ground-floor space.

"They'll be like islands. Folks can wander from one to the other. Can't space them out too much, mind you, or it'll look empty in between."

"Empty? There's two hundred people coming."

"I know it. C'est great!"

". . ."

"Is it really Lionel Arsenault who's paying for all this, then?"

Zed hesitated a moment before replying. "He'd rather we didn't go blabbing it all over town."

"À cause pas?"

Zed shrugged. "He'd rather say it came out of the project's budget. For promotion and such. He's not one to show off."

Pomme straightened one of the trees slightly. "Funny how there's some who'd like nothing better, only they've nothing to show off."

". . ."

"Have you thought about what gift you'll be bringing?"

The invitation stipulated they were to bring nothing more than a small gift, "something cultural."

"I've got something in mind."

Pomme laughed. "Moi itou, don't you know. I can't wait!"

7.
SHI / THE ARMY

THE FIRST FLAKES had begun to fall gently as they approached Peabody. Étienne Zablonski was driving. He liked the name of the place. Meanwhile, Ludmilla was asleep. The radio was playing quietly, as though the snow were blanketing it as well. The forecast was not calling for more than a minor accumulation. Étienne Zablonski slowed down anyway, just to be sure.

A few hours later, in Maine, the situation had changed radically. Sitting straight up, and tense in spite of herself, Ludmilla Zablonski kept her eyes riveted on the snow-covered road ahead. Instead of falling straight down, the snow was blowing horizontally, distorting the surrounding landscape. Once more, Ludmilla suggested they stop. This time Étienne was easily convinced.

The Zablonskis left the main road and ended up in Freeport, where they found a room in a small, rustic inn. The proprietor's warm welcome and the slightly aging charm of the place made them want to dig in and stay a while.

"Did you bring in the books?"

In the lovely dining room, by a crackling fire, the Zablonskis were dining on winter lobster, the innkeeper's specialty, and drinking a smooth Cleebourg Tokay.

"I didn't know there was winter lobster and summer lobster."

The final course was a homemade dessert of cranberries and pears.

While they sipped their coffee, Étienne and Ludmilla Zablonski learned that the storm, which was blowing all the way to Newfoundland, would last another twenty-four hours, at least. It was one of those blizzards rarely seen any more, unpredictable and consequently unpredicted.

"Do you have any cognac?"

Pomme stood in front of the large living-room window, hands on hips, looking outside. This storm, a real howler, had come at the worst possible time — there was still so much to do! In the kitchen, his mother was humming a song while she prepared her meat pies. In her room, his sister was listening to some impossible music. Twice already her father had shouted to turn it down, but it was more a cry for mercy than an affirmation of authority.

The snowplow had not yet cleared their small street. Their neighbour across the way was toiling behind his blower, a useless thing to do in the midst of a snowstorm, Pomme figured, since the wild wind and snow would just as quickly refill the void.

The telephone rang.

"Pomme, it's for you."

Pomme expected to hear Zed's voice on the other end of the line.

"Allô?"

"Pomme? C'est Lisa."

"Oh! Hello! Where are you?"

"In Barachois, though if it keeps on like this, we'll end up in Prince Edward Island before long."

The image made Pomme laugh.

"How is it in Moncton, then?"

"Not too pretty. Even the Tim Hortons are shut down."

"You're joking!"

There followed a moment of silence.

Pomme wasn't sure what to think. "What is it you were wanting?"

"Oh, I don't know really. Just to chat a bit, I suppose."

". . ."

"For one thing, I wanted to say I'm not mad at you."

"Non?"

"Non."

". . ."

"You think we might go for coffee, one of these days? Say in Halifax, or some such place?"

In his bed, little Étienne could stand it no longer. He let out a desperate cry. At least that's how it was perceived by Carmen, who was stretched out on the sofa, immersed in Gérald Leblanc's latest book of poems.

"Terry?"

The legs of the wooden chair on which Terry had been sitting scraped the floor. "Here I go."

Terry had been walking on eggshells ever since Carmen and he had talked. To his surprise, Carmen had virtually come over to his position; at least, she had put up much less opposition. In the end, they had agreed to take some time to think it over. Consequently, Terry was giving her all the time he could.

"Étienne Étienne Étienne Étienne. Comment ça va Étienne Étienne Étienne Étienne . . ."

Carmen smiled to hear him. All things considered, she felt Terry had a rather good paternal instinct. This storm, which had started the day before, had given her the opportunity to confirm it once again.

"Another diaper? Holy gee, Étienne, we gotta talk."

Étienne's good mood was back.

"Eh, Étienne? You and I are going to have to sit down and have a serious man-to-man. That's what we'll do in a bit. We'll go for a beer, you and I, and we'll have a real chat. You'll give me the lowdown. What do you say, Étienne? You'll tell me what sort of dad it is you want. A nappy-changing dad? Is that what you're wanting, then? You want me to win the tournament of nappy-changing dads?"

Étienne was laughing. And so was Carmen.

Pomme braved the storm to get to Zed's home, which was in the same neighbourhood, not far away. On the way, he met absolutely no one, neither car nor pedestrian. That's how bad it was.

When Zed's father opened the door, he was faced with a snow monster. It was only after Pomme removed the scarf hiding his face that Zed's dad recognized him.

"Pomme! It's been a while! I suppose Zed's put you to work as well?"

Later, in Zed's room:

"Your dad sure was in a good mood just now."

"I know it. Seems like he's turned right around lately. He even fixed my truck."

Zed slipped the latest CD by the Païens in the player, and lowered the volume.

"I'm hoping they sell cent milles copies of this CD."

". . ."

"Well, ten thousand, au moins."

They talked of one thing or another for a while, until Pomme steered the conversation over to the topic that was bothering him.

"What would you say if I told you I'd never been out with a girl? In my whole life, I mean."

Zed shrugged. "Nothing wrong with that . . ."

". . ."

Zed wanted to be helpful. "Don't take it wrong, now, but could be you like boys better."

Pomme did not take it badly. "No, that's not it."

". . ."

"It's more like . . . it's as though I can see right through folks."

Zed waited for more.

"It's as though I see behind people, and that's what I like . . . to see how things work from behind, behind the scenes."

". . ."

"And I'm only beginning to see, vraiment."

". . ."

"Is that weird, then?"

Life is a struggle.

    Terry had placed Étienne on the sofa with Carmen, who had begun to read him poems aloud.

> *December. Under December's spell*
> *in the slow pace face to face with white*
> *waiting engenders waiting*
> *a karmic top*
> *unwinds across the land*
> *I patch together all the Decembers of my life*
> *and circle them slowly.*

Something more than silence hung in the air.
"Read that again, will you?"

> *December. Under December's spell*
> *in the slow pace face to face with white*
> *waiting engenders waiting*
> *a karmic top*
> *unwinds across the land*
> *I patch together all the Decembers of my life*
> *and circle them slowly.*

"Mmm . . . Lovely."

    Carmen turned the page, a gesture that never failed to excite Étienne.

> *Equation of fuzziness. Humming of the city*
> *at this hour I . . .*

Terry returned to his Yi Jing, beginning again at the top, because he'd lost track a bit.
7. *The Army. Life is a struggle. Great disorder reigns at this time: take the lead and dedicate yourself to bringing order, take risks, confront obstacles. The changing line in the fourth place indicates that an army needs rest. Calm and patience will triumph even in a troubled relationship. The fifth line, also changing: take your time, avoid following just anyone's advice.*

The two changing lines yielded hexagram 47, *Oppression*, which clearly stated that one should rely on one's own inner light. *A welcome change appears on the horizon and isolation helps to find the way. Love without calculating.*

Terry closed his notebook, put his marbles and books away.

. . . we are in the hands of the immediate of jouissance as the way to expand consciousness . . .

It was not the first time a storm had kept Lionel Arsenault from returning home after a business trip. Sylvia had learned to live with such hibernal contretemps. This time she filled the hours wrapping the gifts Santa Claus would be distributing at the lofts — they were expecting thirty-seven children. Then she baked some dishes for freezing, which she could serve to friends who might show up unexpectedly during the holidays. Afterwards, she went through the house adding decorations here and there. As the storm continued unabated, she reorganized her closet, sewed a few buttons back on, brought in some wood, and let her mind wander while she sorted through the pile of magazines she had tossed into a corner of the living room for the few articles she intended to read one day. In truth, storm or no storm, Sylvia Arsenault was never bored. To her, life was a series of events, all equally interesting, whether big or small. The storm merely wrapped all of it in a cocoon of white silence. The wind, for her, was only the echo of the profound silence of the universe. That morning, Sylvia had prayed to God to make the storm restful and beneficent for all those it touched, even those who did not realize the shelter it provided them. Because, yes, in that sense, she was a believer.

In Maine, daily comings and goings were reduced to a minimum, to the great joy of Étienne and Ludmilla Zablonski. They passed the day reading idly, dozing, delighting in a panoply of delicious appetizers the innkeeper had prepared for them with a pleasure equal to their own. At the end of the day, the Zablonskis took stock.

"In Monk-town, I'll do an analysis."
"Again?"
"No, I mean a kind of study."
"Of what?"
"I don't know. But I feel I have a point of view."
"A point of view?"
". . ."
"Which would be . . . ?"
Ludmilla was in no hurry to clarify her idea; she intended to go on a while longer simply feeling that she had a point of view.

"..."
"..."

"I wonder if human beings were intended for that. To have a point of view."

Although he had the impression he was grasping at shadows, Étienne Zablonski wanted nonetheless to continue the conversation. "Surely someone has already thought about this."

"Surely."

"..."

"Unless, that's what a blizzard does to you."

After supper, Carmen, Terry, and little Étienne found themselves stretched out all together on the couch. The Christmas tree lights illuminated the continuing dance of snowflakes outside the living-room window.

"Terry, are you asleep?"

"No. It's too nice to sleep."

"..."
"..."

"I've been thinking. About the loft, I mean, and all that . . ."

Silently, Terry prepared himself for the worst.

"I swear I don't know why I was so set against it. Now, seems to me, it's a swell idea. Especially since we can each take turns working at the bar, and we'll be in the same building as the kids . . ."

"Vraiment? You agree, then?"

"Don't know what's going on, really: seems like I find it harder and harder to leave Étienne, to go to work and such, I mean. And now, with another one coming . . . Anyhow, I do like the idea of staying close by."

". . ."

"Sometimes, it feels like I'm a long way off from you, too."

Terry gently squeezed Carmen's shoulder. "We're only starting, Belle. We haven't yet got it all under control."

"Funny to think we've only known each other a year and a half."

"Je sais. Feels like years. Not that I mind."

The telephone rang.

"Shall we answer?"

Carmen had only to extend an arm. "Allô?"

"Carmen? Comment ça va? It's Lisa."

"Oh, hello!"

"Is it still blowing in Moncton?"

"Pretty much, yes. And where are you, then?"

"In Barachois, though this afternoon I could have sworn we were about to fly right across to the Island, the way that wind was blowing. It's a bit better now. Comes in gusts. Terry there with you?"

"Sure, hang on a minute . . ."

"No, no! Don't need to talk to him, really. Just tell him for me it works fine when I close my eyes while I'm brushing my teeth. Did he tell you, then?"

"'Bout you getting nauseous and all?"

"Big time! I've been meaning to tell him — I just never think of it when I see him. Pas que I see him all that often, mind you."

"Okay, I'll tell him."
"You still mean to go to the lofts for Christmas?"
"You better believe it."
"All right, then. See you there. When is this tempête supposed to end, anyhow?"
"They don't know, do they. They never saw it coming, and they don't see it going, either."
"I know. Seems like everything's détraqué! And how's Étienne doing?"
"Looks pretty normal to me. He's sleeping just now."
"Oh, cute. Okay, I'll leave you, then. Don't forget to tell Terry."

Terry had already figured it out.

"Funny she would phone just to tell us that."

Terry felt the evening was starting to lose all focus, but he felt no need to steer it back on course. For once, the Yi Jing had failed to provide inspiration.

"It's really great that we feel the same about the loft and the bar and all that . . . But would you mind if we talked about it some other time? Don't know why, I feel fatigué all of a sudden."

"You don't know why? Have you seen yourself? You haven't stopped all day. Really, you're more vaillant than I am in the house."

"You think so, do you?"
"I don't just think so, it's a fact."
"Well, you're working, aren't you. Makes sense."
"Even so . . ."
". . ."

"..."

Terry laid his hand on Carmen's stomach. "Well then? How's la petite these days?"

"Tranquille, seems like. I guess she's resting."

"..."

"And so am I, I suppose."

"C'est ça. Imitating her mom. Already."

20.

GUAN / CONTEMPLATION

THE MAINE BLIZZARD, as Étienne and Ludmilla had dubbed it, had forced a decision on one point at least.

"I prefer the hood with real fur." Ludmilla hesitated. "After all, the fox is already dead. It is fox, isn't it?"

Étienne fingered the fur, and shrugged.

"Do you think it will encourage them to kill more if I buy this one?"

Étienne was being realistic. "It's quite possible."

Ludmilla made her decision regardless; she gripped the parka with the hood trimmed in real fur under her arm and put the other one back.

"After all, I eat meat, don't I?"

Étienne, meanwhile, had already picked out his wardrobe. Ludmilla had never seen him wearing so many colours at once.

"Bravo, I think you're only missing pink."

Étienne laughed. At the cash, he added a pair of rose-tinted sunglasses to his pile.

At the lofts, there was much to do to make up the time lost due to the storm.

"Pomme, is this where you'll be wanting the big tables?"

"Don't know yet. All depends on the electricians."

"At what time do they get here, then?"

"Don't know, do I. They ought to be here déjà."

Pomme had quite naturally taken charge of the loft Christmas project. Even Zed was under his orders.

"Have you found mattresses?"

"Salvation Army's sending them over après-midi."

"You'll put them in the corner là-bas, then, and you can hang this around them, to make a sort of curtain."

The cloth in question was, in fact, no more than a veil.

"It's just to make une petite division. And c'est fireproof, by the way."

"And where did you find it?"

Pomme did not have time to answer.

"Pomme, the electricians are here. Can they begin with the DJ's corner?"

Terry had described for Carmen the small work of art, absolutely appropriate for the occasion, that he had found in Mathieu Léger's studio.

"He said he'd give me a good price. But how can we make certain Zed's the one who gets it? Will folks be picking up just any cadeau? Or will someone be handing them out, you think? That way, I could arranger ça with the one who's doing the handing out."

"Probably best if someone's handing them out. Unless, when it's Zed's turn, you pull out your gift and give it to him, on behalf of everyone."

"Bonne idée!"

". . ."

"And what about Lionel Arsenault, then? Oughtn't we to have something special for him, as well?"

"There's that, too, I suppose."

"Actually, there were two oeuvres like this. Not exactly pareilles, but with the picture of the building, I mean."

". . ."

"Although, two might be trop cher. Unless Mathieu gives us a price for two."

"Especially if he knows who they're meant for."

Sylvia had gone over to Annette's to help prepare a few select dishes that simply couldn't be entrusted to the caterer.

"There's some folks that don't care for allspice and there's some for whom it's just not Christmas without it. So, quoi faire?"

"Put it in."

Annette felt that Sylvia saw things clearly. "You're so right. After all, c'est Noël. It's now or never, I suppose."

Annette tossed in a healthy dose of allspice, stirred the pot, and invited Sylvia to have a taste.

"Mmm . . . Really good!"

Sylvia surprised herself, as a matter of fact, because normally she was one of those people who didn't like allspice. But she preferred not to say so.

"Really?"

"Really. It's just right."

Her sincerity was convincing, and it multiplied Annette's joy tenfold.

Content with the deal he had struck for the two art pieces destined for Zed and Lionel Arsenault, Terry, with little Étienne in tow, made his way down Botsford Street to Dooly's on Main, to show his acquisitions to Carmen. At first, she was not overly enthusiastic.

"I like those Scrabble letters. And the little holes. The little nails, as well."

20. Contemplation. Represents both the act of contemplating and the situation of being contemplated, and all possibilities between the two.

"Yeah. It is kind of nice. Could be you have to get used to it."

"I'd say Zed's going to like it."

"Anyhow, it's a swell idea, if only on account of the photograph. And because it's Mathieu."

Carmen, who had been fussing over Étienne a bit, didn't want to see him go quite yet. "I wouldn't mind if you two waited for me. We could go together."

Terry was happy to oblige. But rather than waiting there — the hexagram had also spoken of acting freely, without concern for time — he decided to take a walk past the boutiques on Main Street and come back an hour later, when Carmen would be ready to go. It was Christmas Eve, after all.

"Eh, Étienne? After all, c'est quasiment Noël. Can't go home without seeing what's doing on Main!"

Father and son went into a few boutiques. Terry was thinking he might pick up a surprise for Carmen, since she'd already guessed her other presents. It was a bit difficult to extricate Étienne from the sled each time and to wander up and down the aisles with the child in his arms. He did it three times before giving up. Anyway, he only had twenty minutes left.

Étienne and Ludmilla Zablonski were quietly enjoying their coffee, Ludmilla leafing absent-mindedly through a magazine she'd picked up at random.

"Do you believe in spontaneous change?"

Étienne had never really thought about it, but he had nothing against it.

Ludmilla continued to turn the pages.

"It is true that strategies can end up being rather burdensome."

Étienne wondered just what magazine she was looking at.

"It must be possible to be neither searching for nor running away from something . . ."

Étienne also thought this possible.

"Without things being static."

With these words, Ludmilla lifted her eyes from the magazine to see Étienne's face transformed.

25.

WU WANG / WITHOUT GUILE

PEOPLE WERE ARRIVING in a steady stream, happily but unhurriedly shedding their outer clothing. Pomme noted that they had been wise to reserve a large area for boots and coats. He was equally satisfied to see that the youngsters charged with welcoming people — wearing sparkling elf suits — had taken their task to heart.

"And my name's Nadine, if you ever need help finding your things . . ."

But it was really only once they approached the centre of the great hall that people could appreciate the full effect of what had been accomplished. Zed's mother, in particular, was overflowing with compliments.

"Will you look at that!"

The Christmas tree hanging upside down from the ceiling looked like a giant candelabra.

"Isn't that lovely? Who could have thought of such a thing?"

"Was Pomme, actually, and a couple of others, who had most of the ideas."

"Pomme, was it? Well, isn't that the way of things. Someone's tranquille like that, you can bet there's a whole lot going on upstairs."

As the Christmas presents began to pile up around the trees, the excitement of the children mounted.

"No, no, little devil, mustn't touch."

"Zed, I want you to meet Étienne and Ludmilla."

Zed shook hands with the guests. Terry had already told him on the phone how he'd bumped into the couple at the Grabbajabba café.

"It's an honour to meet you. Terry still can't get over you being here in Moncton."

"Well, you have to admit, what were the chances we'd see him again? I mean, someone you meet like that, en voyage in Europe . . ."

"You're a painter, then, are you?"

"I guess you could say so."

Zed wanted also to say something to Ludmilla, who looked fabulously gorgeous.

"And you?"

"I used to work in publishing."

"You're on holiday, then? Folks usually come around here during the summer . . ."

Ludmilla replied quite naturally. "We wanted to experience your blizzards."

Zed had a sudden flash. "Do you know Leonard Cohen, the singer?"

"Of course. Why? Is he coming tonight?"

Zed burst out laughing. "No, it's just that you mentioned blizzards. That made me think of him."

Although Lionel Arsenault had no desire to be the centre of attention, everyone awaited his arrival eagerly. It would confirm that he was really Zed's right arm, or vice versa.

Aunt Annette spoke with some authority on the subject. "Sylvia told me this afternoon they'd be arriving around ten-thirty. They were going by to see her mother for a bit first."

This was pretty much what Lionel had told Zed.

"Won't they be attending Mass, as well?"

"Most likely. Anyhow, I can't wait to see Sylvia's reaction. She won't believe her eyes."

"C'est vrai, it's beautiful. I'm impressed myself."

People mingled easily. They joined in with conversations or started up new ones that would then move on from one cluster to the next.

"Who's that with Terry and Carmen over there?"

"Can't say. I'm sure I don't know them."

"I thought it might be Lionel Arsenault and his wife."

"No, that's not them."

"The fellow's pas mal beau, just the same."

"She's not exactly hard to look at, herself."

"No, but look, he's au moins as handsome as John Cassavetes."

"I tell you, ça sparkle big time à soir."

"Well, c'est Noël, non? It's normal que ça sparkle."

Those children that still believed, or wanted to believe, in Santa Claus could fall asleep on the mattresses, thereby giving him time to climb down the chimney and have his cookies and milk, according to custom.

"What's going on over there, then?"

"They're telling Christmas stories to the kids, pour les endormir."

"And they're listening?"

". . ."

"Well, it gives the parents a break, I suppose."

Terry had had to lie down with the children, because Étienne was too small to stay by himself. The baby wasn't too sure what was going on. But once Terry had the bright idea to give Étienne a book and get him turning the pages, the boy understood someone was telling a story. Terry proudly related this to Carmen, Étienne, and Ludmilla.

"That little one won't just go listening to any old story. He has to be turning the pages on his own."

Zed did not want to monopolize Lionel Arsenault, but there were a number of people to whom he wanted to introduce him.

"Dad, this is Lionel Arsenault and his wife, Sylvia."

Zed's father extended a hand. "Glad to meet you."

"I hear you've a small business yourself?"

"Oh, it's not much. Me and a couple of guys, we do some welding."

Lionel Arsenault was interested. "Well, now I see where Zed gets it — taking all sorts of things and putting them together, I mean."

The response made Zed's father smile, but it also made him proud. Especially when Zed added, "Hey! C'est vrai ça! I never thought of it that way."

"Mélanie! I thought you'd gone to Mexico!" Sylvia was always happy to see Lisa-M.

"No . . . Everyone was so excited about having Christmas here, I figured, well . . . C'est beau, non? Have you seen the corner over there, with the sofas and the fireplace?"

"A fireplace?"

"Well, not a real one, though you can barely tell. You can only be really sure when you put your hand through the fire and it doesn't burn."

"!"

"I can't wait to see the lofts. I wouldn't mind one myself. They're saying they won't be all that expensive. I know beaucoup de monde who'd like to live here already . . . Isn't the music swell? Bosse's brother's the DJ. He's a whole lot better at it than Bosse."

"Is it Ti-Len's boys, Jean-Pierre and Luc, you're talking about, then?"

Somehow Sylvia managed to keep track of the young people and their nicknames.

"Have you met the couple from the States? They're pretty chic, wouldn't you say?"

"I thought they were from Europe . . ."

"I know, their French sure does sound like le français de France."

Most of the adults watched Santa Claus distribute the gifts to the children, although several small groups continued their conversations.

"Is it true, then, Leonard Cohen's supposed to show up? That's what one girl over there heard."

"Quelle fille?"
"And what would Leonard Cohen be doing around here, I'd like to know."
"Right. À part de ça, he's Jewish, don't you know."
"I thought he was Zen."
"Either way . . ."
"I thought Zen believers could do pretty well anything they liked."
"I don't know, do I. I'm only repeating what I've heard."
"Mistake."
". . ."
"Are you saying Jews don't celebrate Noël? That's dur à croire . . ."

Étienne and Ludmilla were following the adults' exchange of gifts with great interest. They did not know that the type of presents had been specified in the invitation.
Ludmilla turned to her husband. "They're awfully sophisticated, don't you think?"
To Étienne, the entire evening had been a series of surprises.
"*The Red Gospel* by . . . Holy shit! Who the hell is this? Wys . . . chienne . . . grade . . . ski . . ."
"Wyschnegradsky!"
The correct pronunciation, shouted from somewhere in the back of the hall, made everyone laugh.
Terry's brother continued to examine the CD box.
Someone else shouted, "I'll take it if you don't want it!"
"Well, I suppose I'll give it a listen at least once, first . . ."
Zed's cousin was next. She chose a present in the shape

of a bottle — there had already been some vintage wines, expensive olive oil, and real balsamic vinegar — and unwrapped it.

"I'm sure I don't know what it is. There's nothing written on it."

Someone, trying to help her out, picked up the wrapping paper and searched for a tag of some sort.

"Open it, why don't you?"

Which she did.

"En tout cas, sure smells good."

At last someone got it.

"It's shampoo from Colette's."

The word went around.

"What's that, you say?"

"Shampoo, from chez Colette."

"And what's culturel about that, I'd like to know."

"It's a concept store in Paris."

"Oh."

At four in the morning, Terry was sprawled on the end of a couch, Étienne asleep in his arms. Beside him, Carmen had joined a game of Trivial Pursuit. The rules were not particularly clear; nevertheless, everyone, including the Zablonskis, was trying hard to win.

"This one's for Terry. Terry, are you asleep?"

"Yes and no."

"In the Yi Jing, what's the name of hexagram 25?"

"You're joking!"

"Non, non, c'est vrai!"

"I don't believe it."

Carmen got up to show Terry the card. It was indeed true.

"Well, believe it or not, it's 'Simplicité.' 'Without Guile,' in English, and that's the one I got this very morning."

The reaction was unanimous: "Nonnn!"

"I'm telling you! That's why I didn't believe you."

"Incroyable, indeed!"

"'A movement following the law of heaven,' it said. And that's exactly what it is."

15.

QIAN / MODESTY

"That surprises me."

"What is it that surprises you?"

A fellow Terry had seen around but didn't know had pulled up a chair to join the conversation. Terry pushed aside the baby's gear to make room and waited for the man to sit down.

"The other night, on TV-France, there was a québecoise singer talking about just this song. She said she'd met a guy from Moncton who told her his grand-mère used to sing it to him."

"So?"

"Well, she never said Moncton en Acadie, or Moncton, New Brunswick, or any such thing. As though everybody and his uncle knew where Moncton was."

". . ."

"As though we were une grande ville or some well-known place."

". . ."

"En tout cas, it surprised me."

The guy who'd just sat down did not appear to have a firm opinion on the subject.

"And who was this singer?"

"Mara Tremblay. You don't forget a name like that."

". . ."

"Come to think of it, you wouldn't really forget the girl non plus." The fellow pronounced what seemed like his conclusion on the subject: "I'm wondering who the fellow was she met."

And he added, with a gesture of impatience, "Are they not serving coffee in here any more, ou quoi?"

The Prizon Art movement — the "z" representing a kind of minuscule homage to Zablonski — was an enormous success, both in terms of the speed with which it spread and the density of the works it spawned. The art critic who discovered it (two of his brothers were inmates at the same penitentiary as the Zablonskian pyromaniac) spoke of the movement with such fervour that he triggered a minor stampede on the gates of the prison in question.

Minuscule homage to Zablonski, because the prisoners did not intend to praise anyone or thing at all. Stubborn diehards that they were, they certainly did not want to demonstrate that it was possible to be emancipated in prison. Repeatedly they insisted that they had been initiated into painting in spite of themselves, and that they were now practising the art by compulsion — in other words, as a result of intense exposure to a painting by Étienne Zablonski. Although they realized that they were thereby granting a painting enormous powers, they much preferred this to crediting the system that had branded them criminals.

On his way home, Terry began to feel that winter had overstayed its welcome. And yet, earlier, on his way to the café, he had been marvelling at the scintillating white that covered everything and at the large snowbanks that continued to block the view from entrances and street corners. No, he couldn't remember a winter with so many blizzards — he pronounced the word à la française, the way Ludmilla did.

Terry turned to glance back at Étienne, comfortably ensconced in the sled.

"Eh, Étienne? What do you think, then? Are folks fed up ou quoi?"

The snow deposited by successive storms had severely narrowed the streets, and a good number of sidewalks had not been cleared. As a result, Terry looked behind him quite a bit as he moved forward. Several times he was forced to clamber up a snowbank to allow cars to go by. As a rule, these were not going very fast, but they occasionally skidded to the right or left on the layer of ice and snow that covered the pavement.

"You'll remember to fix all this, won't you, Étienne, when you're maire de Moncton?"

Zed and Zablonski took their break along with the other workers on the construction site. This afternoon, they were standing off to one side, chatting.

"Funny how both our names start with Z."

Zablonski agreed. "Is that your real given name?"

Zed laughed. "Jokes-tu?"

". . ."

"The first truly good thing I did in my life was to change my name."

". . ."

"And you?"

"Me?"

"Oui. What's a vraiment bonne chose you've done in your life?"

The question required some thought, or at least a kind of introspection of which Zablonski had lost the habit. Instead, he replied in kind: "Jokes-tu?"

Zed decided Étienne was acclimatizing well.

15. Modesty. Put aside pride and complications and live your love fully. It is time for clarity: speak in simple words and do not abandon the Yi Jing. Choose the inferior rank but be alert because relationships beckon. The changing line in the second place indicates that you will be entrusted with important responsibilities, precisely because your modesty inspires confidence. Take advantage of this and make a wish from the bottom of your heart; it will come true.

Terry hesitated to make a wish from the bottom of his heart. Would his wish be sufficiently inspired? He pushed his chair back, stretched his legs, closed his eyes, and tried to relax. It was not always easy to abandon one's pride and complications. What's more, was he required to make his wish immediately? He decided that nothing compelled him to do so; he could let it simmer for a while, a few hours anyway, maybe even a day or two. He completed his divination: the changing line yielded hexagram 46,

Pushing Upward. The foundation is solid and your goal is in harmony with your surroundings and society, you are on the right path. Work hard, fear not, your time will come. Do not hesitate to go see the great man.
The telephone rang. It was Carmen.
"Oh, nothing much."
Terry immediately corrected himself, remembering that he was to speak clearly, from the bottom of his heart.
"Pour dire le vrai, I'm just finishing my Yi Jing."
"And?"
"Looks good . . ."
He added, so as to express his love fully, "For all of us, I mean. Notre famille."
Carmen had gone in to work early in the afternoon. She hadn't really felt like it, but, as manager, she felt it her duty to participate in all the employees' committee meetings. She had taken advantage of a break to call home.
"And Étienne, how's he, then?"
"Sleeping. I took him along to the café tantôt . . . I don't know if it's on account of the last storm, but le monde was grouchy là-bas."
". . ."
"They were getting pissed off for nothing."
". . ."
"Ça fait que we didn't hang about for long."

The Zablonskis were settling down in Acadia — in Moncton, to be exact — but they had not yet entirely realized it. Since their arrival, they had found nothing more to do than respond to the natural appeal of the town and its people.

"We'll go farther north next winter, perhaps as far as Nunavut."

Zed was already loath to think of their leaving, but he didn't quite know how to say so.

"Mmm . . ."

For the time being, the couple was camping in a livable space of the lofts under construction, in exchange for some conceptual work by Zablonski, who had a real talent for surfaces and textures.

"In any case, we can't stay here forever."

Zed shrugged. "And why not, pray tell?"

"To settle down again?"

Zed couldn't see what the problem was.

Later that evening, on the telephone again:

"Are you saying I speak too much Chiac?"

"Seems like it's gotten worse lately. It's as though you're doing it on purpose."

"On purpose? Moi? What are you talking about?"

Terry was trying to get his bearings by recalling the Yi Jing. The oracle had said to use simple words, but it hadn't specified in which language. Terry needed to think, whereas Carmen seemed to have already thought it out.

"I'm thinking of Étienne. It's not very nice, a child speaking Chiac. It's not as bad when it's an adult."

". . . ?"

Terry hadn't seen any of this coming. And, he had to admit, he was hurt.

"Geeze, Carmen, you surprise me, you do. We've never talked about this. About how we speak. I mean, that it might be a problem."

"Well, don't take it badly. We'll talk about it some more. Must be on account of the kids. I suppose it makes me think about stuff I never thought about before."

Since he'd received a book about avant-garde art at the lofts' Christmas party, Pomme had become fascinated with the subject. It was not, therefore, mere coincidence that he learned of the Prizon Art movement, because recently he had taken to browsing through the art journals over at Reid's and in the university library.

"Those guys don't care, man. They're embarrés, and they've got nothing else to do but paint all day long, until they pass right à travers those walls."

"What? You mean to say they're scraping the walls? I'm surprised they let them do it . . ."

"I would have thought it was the thickness of the paint qui comptait . . ."

"Not just that. You have to give the colours time to settle."

"What does that do, pray tell?"

No one knew for sure.

"Ça fait que, so what?"

"Ça fait que, it all started with this fellow, un pyromaniac, who burned down the house of an artist."

"Where did this happen, then?"

"Aux States."

"Figures."

"Puis après?"

Pomme had finally arrived at the nub of his story. He did not want to miss the punchline.

"Well, see, the artist's name was Zablonski. Étienne Zablonski."

Astonishment all around.

"You're joking!"

"I am not joking. It's written right là." Pomme flipped open his journal, showed them the page.

The others looked at each other.

"And Terry knows all this, I suppose, and he never breathed a word?"

Pomme let the conversation flow without interrupting.

"À cause wouldn't he have told us? It's no great secret, is it?"

". . ."

"He must know. Même que the kid's named Étienne on account of him."

"Is that right? I didn't know that."

"Me neither."

"Well sure! He bought un diamond à Carmen, and everything!"

"Who did?"

"Zablonski."

"Quoi? He wanted to marry her?"

"When was that?"

"Well, quoi? Don't the lot of you know anything at all?"

55.
FENG / ABUNDANCE

"I THOUGHT YOU liked my way of talking Chiac. That was one of the first things you said to me when we met."

"Well, sure, I liked it. Only now it's different, isn't it."

Terry plunged in. "All right, I can see the point of it, I mean, if you know the word. I wouldn't mind saying poêlonne instead of frying pan. But what about when you don't know the French word? Like ball bearing, for example. Or steering wheel."

"You don't know how to say steering wheel in French?" Carmen was trying not to lose patience, but she felt it was high time to have it out.

"Well, maybe I do know it. Still, it's not a word I'd actually be using at the garage, is it?" Terry said, letting slip the word "using" in English. "All depends on who it is you're talking to, I suppose."

Carmen exploded. "You see? Right there, you said 'using,' in English. How is it you couldn't say the other thing? You couldn't say 'utiliser'? Well, that's exactly what I mean! You'd think you were doing it on purpose!"

". . ."

"You're not trying very hard, and that's for certain."

". . ."

"I mean, your French was a whole lot better when we were in France."

"Well, that was different. They didn't know us in France, did they. Anyway, I didn't talk so much over there."

". . ."

"And since when do we have to work so hard to speak our language? I mean, whose language is it? Can't we speak our own language the way we want to?"

". . ."

"Je veux dire, is it really de quoi we've got to be fretting about right here and now?"

Pomme was more than a little proud to have dug up Étienne Zablonski's background. To him, it seemed as though he'd made a scientific discovery. Even Hermé, who was usually right on top of the latest trends, had to admit he had not heard of the Prizon Art movement.

"Must be awfully recent."

Pomme opened the magazine to display the article entitled "The Isolated Ones." Hermé immediately had something to say, based on the title alone.

"Hmm. Harkens back to Georges-Albert Aurier's article on Van Gogh in the first issue of the *Mercure de France*, in 1890."

Quickly he scanned the article, while Pomme stood there waiting in the middle of the hallway of the Aberdeen Centre. It was as though thousands of connections were lighting up in Hermé's head as he was reading, and Pomme loved to watch it.

Aunt Annette and Sylvia Arsenault had taken a liking to Ludmilla. What's more, they couldn't get over the fact of being friends with an actual squatter.

"You should have told me. I'd have gone over to fetch you."

Ludmilla had walked from the laundromat to the restaurant where the three women had agreed to meet. When she'd stepped in the door, the waiter had offered to put her large canvas sack full of freshly washed clothes under the cash counter.

"It was a last-minute thing, really. Generally, I do my wash at Terry and Carmen's. That way, I can babysit Étienne at the same time — he's such a lovely child. You might say it's a matter of striking two birds with one stone."

How beautifully she spoke! To Sylvia's ears, it was like a gentle stream flowing. It made her want to warble likewise.

"Is it true, then, that they named him Étienne after your husband? That's what I heard . . ."

Though she did her best to enunciate clearly, Sylvia could not hear such music in her own speech. Worse, she was sure she was making mistakes. When you talked, there was no chance to double back.

"Yes, that is true, though it's a long story."

"Do we look as though we're in a hurry, then?"

Ludmilla told them what she knew, which made a big impression on Annette.

"Well, if that isn't the most incredible thing! Would you believe such a coincidence was possible?"

"As a matter of fact, we did know — rather, I should say, Étienne knew — that they, Terry and Carmen, were from

Monk-town. In a strange sort of way, that's what lured us here."

Lured. Sylvia was in awe of Ludmilla's vocabulary. Annette, on the other hand, was more astonished by the coincidences of fate.

"Well, still, just think of it! To meet like that! On Main Street! And three days before Christmas!"

Ludmilla could not deny it. "Yes, Étienne was overjoyed. And so was I, by ricochet."

Ricochet! Such beauty gave Sylvia goosebumps. And it seemed so easy. It stirred something deep within her.

"I'm telling you, I just kind of blew up." Terry looked absolutely dejected.

"Well, why don't you just say you're sorry and be done with it?"

"And what do you think I did?"

"Well then? How did she take it?"

"Pas trop pire . . ."

". . ."

"I suppose she didn't want to stay enragée any more than I did."

". . ."

"Still, I can't seem to shake it. Je comprends pas the why of it."

"Could be you're both stressed, or some such thing. You've got a whole lot of stuff going on, haven't you. And with Carmen pregnant, encore de plus."

"Je sais. But they're all things we want to do."

Zed understood, and he had no desire to lose Terry, his

confidant and strong right arm — after Lionel Arsenault, of course, who was, in truth, more than an arm . . . more like a crane!

"Ça fait que, what was this argument about, anyway?"

Terry shook his head. "You won't believe it. It was about Chiac."

"Chiac?"

Again Terry shook his head. Zed waited for more.

"Carmen thinks I ought to try harder, to speak a better French, I mean. On account of the boy. And the girl that's on the way."

". . ."

"She thinks it's not nice for a kid to speak Chiac."

Zed thought for a moment. "I can see her point."

Terry was not surprised. "And moi itou, don't you know! But what would you have us do about all those things we don't even know the words for in French?"

"Such as?"

"Such as, I don't know, all sorts of things . . . roller blinds."

Zed tried, but he came up blank. Nevertheless, after a moment his face brightened. "Well, just imagine, can't you? What if they made Chiac like cigarettes and booze? You wouldn't be allowed to speak it until you were nineteen." Zed burst out laughing. He really liked the idea, even if it was his own.

After a moment, he said, "What are you up to now? I mean, is Carmen expecting you back?"

"No. Étienne's off in Dieppe, and Carmen's gone to work early."

Zed stood up. "Parfait! Viens. Won't take long. We'll go take a look at something."

In the truck, Terry was thinking aloud:

"It's funny. Our worst fights — between Carmen and me, I mean — Étienne's never been home. Wonder if she plans it that way. If it continues on comme ça, whenever I know Étienne's not going to be around, I'll start to worry."

A few minutes passed.

"One thing for sure, now I know why it is they call it the mother tongue."

Pomme was in a good mood and, at the same time, slightly overexcited. The hours he'd spent in the Champlain Library had both stimulated and exhausted him. He felt a need to talk, but not to just anyone.

"Lisa?"

"Pomme?"

"I was just wondering what you were up to."

"Well, to be honest, I was just about to bust my flute in two."

"Great! How'd you like to come out for a beer instead? We'll chat a bit and then you can bust it, if you still feel like it."

"Bonne idée!"

"Only problem, I won't have time to take you to Halifax or anything like that."

"Who cares?"

"Carmen just won't believe this . . ."

Terry and Zed emerged from the Librairie Acadienne,

their arms full of dictionaries. After consulting with the salesperson, they'd selected: the two-volume set of the *Petit Robert* (not all that petit, in Terry's view), one volume for common nouns, naturally, and the other for proper nouns (might as well, Zed figured); the *Robert-Collins* French-English; and the bilingual *Visuel* dictionaries. Zed paid for everything, a gift, he said, for all the help Terry had given him.

"Surtout the one with the pictures. There at least you can see what le monde is made of."

"That's the truth! I should have bought one for my sisters, as well."

They piled the dictionaries on the front seat between them, and Terry began to leaf through *Le Visuel* while Zed went back into the bookstore to buy another one for his sisters.

On the road, Terry added, in spite of himself, "Well, but it's awfully expensive quand même. Not everyone could afford something like this."

"Everything costs nowadays . . . Everything."

"Don't I know it. But paying for your own langue, well, that's a bit much."

That evening, Ludmilla recounted her meeting with Annette and Sylvia to Étienne.

"They wanted to know which loft we were planning to buy."

"What did you say?"

"That we didn't know yet."

". . ."

"There was something in the way they looked at me . . ."

". . ."

"Something . . . I don't know. I can't quite put my finger on it."

". . ."

"There are lapses in this country, don't you find?"

"Lapses?"

"Yes. Lapses. Gaps . . . or slippage, both in space and in time."

". . ."

"No?"

Étienne Zablonski drew close to his wife, put an arm around her, and planted a kiss in her soft, supple hair.

Ludmilla continued, "And what exactly would we do in Nunavut?"

Carmen would be arriving any minute. Terry was so excited he could hardly concentrate. He'd cleared a space on a shelf in their increasingly encumbered apartment and lined up the dictionaries. Little Étienne had already been initiated. Now he was babbling away in his playpen.

55. Abundance. Your cup is overflowing, almost to excess. You are replete with talent and success, surrounded by friends and riches. Enjoy their support and generosity now, they are the fruits of your past actions. The harvest is abundant, rejoice, although the cycle is coming to an end. Shine like the midday sun.

Terry digested this initial information, rose, rewound Étienne's musical toy, and went out to the kitchen to pour himself a beer.

128

The changing line in the first place encouraged him to put aside his timidity and to approach an important person as his equal, because the association that would emerge from their meeting would benefit both parties. As for the second changing line, in the third position, it announced a paralyzing profusion — the loss of a supporter, like a broken right hand — but nothing too serious.

Terry swallowed a mouthful of beer before moving on to the linked hexagram.

16. Enthusiasm. Take pleasure in thinking through your plan and creating the conditions for harmony. Rely on wisdom and prepare yourself for the time when you must react spontaneously, because it will be wonderful! Like a child riding an elephant.

"Zablonski? Are you there?"

It must have been around nine in the evening when Étienne Zablonski heard this unexpected shout. He got up and went to the large window. He could see nothing special down below. Then he heard knocking on one of the doors of the warehouse under renovation.

"Zablonski? C'est Zed!"

Étienne Zablonski saw three figures backing away from the base of the building. Two of them were carrying bags. The trio was looking up, in the direction of the section of the building where Ludmilla and he had moved in. Étienne recognized Zed.

"Zablonski? It's Zed! I'm here with Pomme and Lisa-Minnelli! We've come to visit!"

Zed could have entered the building — he had all the

keys — but, not wishing to frighten the Zablonskis, and also because this time he'd come as a visitor, he felt it proper to behave as a guest. Or, at least, as one who might be welcomed as a guest.

64.

WEI JI / BEFORE COMPLETION

"You've no need to worry about l'anonymat round here. You'll have plenty of that."
Pomme had brought along his magazine and shown it to Étienne Zablonski.
Off in a corner, Lisa-M. was dancing on her own to an unrecognizable tune playing on the old ghetto blaster Zed had lent the Zablonskis. Ludmilla watched the dance carefully, in case it would help her name this clearly perceivable yet indefinable thing she was feeling.
"I've never been, nor am I now, the type to start off a trend." Zablonski laughed, adding, "I'm more the type that breaks away."
Pomme listened intently to the famous artist. He was surprised to discover that he knew what an art world trend-setter was — all that stuff he'd been reading actually did have a basis in reality!
"Funny that Van Gogh started painting when he lost his job. I mean, he was fired, right? Set on fire. Allumé, you might say."
Zablonski was at once amused and intrigued by Pomme, who was pouring wine all around. When their glasses were full, he handed the bottle to Zablonski, to read the label.

"It's only recently we've started getting all worked up about the wine we drink around here."

Zed added, "C'est vrai ça. It's gotten so even I sniff it before I drink."

All three turned to watch the dancing Lisa-M., who at that moment, perhaps coincidentally, had become particularly graceful. For a while, no one said another word.

Carmen came home later than usual that evening.

"I'm awfully tired. Don't know how long I'll be able to carry this baby."

Terry took her coat and scarf and shook them off before hanging them in the closet, because it had started to snow again.

"And anything new 'round here?"

To Terry she seemed particularly gentle, vulnerable.

"Well, I've been thinking over that whole Chiac business. And, well, I can see what you're saying. Since then, I can't help hearing myself every time I use an English word. It sounds twice as loud in my head."

In vain, Terry had sought a way to bring Zed into his story without offending Carmen. In the end, he decided to be direct.

"And I spoke to Zed about it, who, by the way, was on your side."

Terry realized too late he'd used the English "by the way," but this was no time to flinch. He got up and crossed over to the shelf where he'd placed the dictionaries.

"So . . . Zed's given us a present."

Carmen saw the four volumes.

Terry made a formal presentation: "Common nouns, proper nouns, French-English — or English-French, don't know for sure how you're supposed to say it — and . . ." Terry pulled out *Le Visuel* and brought it over to Carmen, opening it at random. "See . . . here's the word in French and in English."

". . ."

"Like here, for instance, I thought this thing here was a footstool," he said, using the English term. "But turns out it's a pouf. And a footstool is a tabouret in French. Stepstool, chaise escabeau; beanbag, fauteuil-sac; stacking chairs, chaises empilables; folding chair, chaise pliante . . . well, we knew that one, didn't we."

Terry flipped to another page at random. He landed on edible shellfish and scanned the page quickly before exclaiming, "Well, we know quite a bit on this page . . . And look at this, will you? What we call couteaux are really couteaux!"

Now it was Carmen's turn to leaf through the book. The electric clothes dryer, or sécheuse, caught her eye. She picked out several other appliances.

"Well . . ."

Then, flipping over a big chunk of pages, her eye fell on office supplies, which she studied more carefully, finally pointing to one item and declaring, "That's exactly what I wanted! A clamp binder! Didn't even know how to say it in English!"

Terry pulled the dictionary over toward him a bit, to see. Carmen showed him the item.

"Reliure à pince. I know. That's what's si great. Toutes ces choses we didn't know the names for. And don't you just love the colours, the drawings?"

They continued to leaf through the dictionary without really reading, just to see. Then Carmen closed the book to have a look at the cover, after which she turned her gaze to the other volumes along the shelf.

"Sure, it's a super gift . . ."

Terry breathed a sigh of relief.

At the Zablonskis, the evening had increasingly taken on the appearance of a party.

"The Moncton Accidents! The way you put it, I imagined a hockey team . . . sponsored by an insurance company."

Zed was annoyed with himself for not having found the French word for "sponsored." Terry and Carmen's dispute had affected him. Usually, even when he didn't use the French word, at least he knew it.

Pomme continued along his own train of thought. "Well, c'est vrai, though. C'est comme si I've got a whole slew of photos already taken in my head. The door opens, a woman comes out half bent over, the front of the car half smashed in. Ou le gros truck half tippé under the overpass on Main. Everything's like à moitié. Cayouche found a swell title for his CD: Moitié-moitié. Half-and-half. Although I've no idea if it's related in any way."

Étienne and Ludmilla were taking it all in, in silence.

"Moi, it's cutting my toenails does it. Days I cut my toenails, if I do nothing else, I've done a lot."

"Are they that thick, then?" Zed had merely wanted to make a joke. He hadn't expected Lisa-M. to reply.

"No. Don't know why, really. C'est comme ça, I suppose."

Zed thought about it seriously for a moment. "Must be the animal in you . . . as though you were really losing something of yourself."

Lisa-M. gave Zed a long, questioning look.

"En tout cas, you've got something with your body. It's obvious just à voir la way que tu danses. And aren't you the one had trouble brushing your teeth?"

"Terry told you that?"

"Guess what I was thinking earlier today."

Lionel Arsenault always enjoyed hearing what his wife was thinking.

"That we should buy one of those lofts."

The idea made Lionel laugh. Sylvia was not offended.

"Sounds crazy, I know . . ."

The idea was more surprising than crazy to Lionel. From the start of the project, he had never imagined himself and Sylvia living there.

"Sometimes I wish we lived in town. I could take courses at the university . . ."

"We don't have to move into town for that."

"I know . . ." Sylvia adjusted the pillow and leaned against her husband's shoulder.

"What sort of courses, then?"

"Don't know. I suppose I wouldn't mind taking photography."

"Really?"

"And there's something about French, too. The way the words hold everything together somehow."

"Really!"

Pomme was funny to watch and listen to. Even Zed and Lisa-M. had never seen him in quite this light.

"You ask me, we're not vraiment ready for art. We don't really know how to approach it. There's, like, something missing. You can have all the museums you like, there's something missing."

". . ."

"It's full of contradictions, isn't it? Really, c'est plus comme an addiction. Which is not what people think it is, you know. Folks think an addiction is an addiction. But in fact, it's a neutralizer. Contradiction/neutraddiction. Get it?"

Pomme poured himself another glass of wine.

"Don't mind me, folks."

And he looked at the label on the bottle.

"Vraiment, this wine's not bad."

"I thought the lofts would be a place to help out artists. Not for rich folks who just want . . ." Lionel Arsenault realized he was about to say something that would hurt his wife. "Well, if it was bigger, I suppose there'd be room for all sorts of folks. As it is . . ."

"I wouldn't want anything very big . . ."

". . ."

"Même, I'd prefer something small, really. Just a small place in town. And for the photography, it wouldn't be all that complicated. Everything's done with computers these days."

The businessman tried to imagine Sylvia living the Bohemian life — techno-Bohemian, to boot.

Sylvia did not feel like talking too much about her idea, which was perhaps already a project. "Really, I love the way Ludmilla talks, I do. She says words like 'lured' and 'ricochet.'"

Lionel Arsenault felt the word ricochet in his head. "Yes, 'ricochet' is nice."

And he fell asleep on the soft bounce of the word.

"Carmen!" Zed was surprised and happy to see Carmen again. He gave her a big hug, and felt the roundness of her tummy. "And how did you folks know we were here?"

"Well, you weren't at home, or at L'Osmose . . . So, we just drove by here and we spotted your truck."

This time Terry used the French "camion." He'd felt the English word "truck" rising in his throat, but he'd replaced it in time.

"Pomme and Lisa-M. are upstairs."

Terry had figured Pomme would go see Zablonski to talk about the article. "Well? And what did Zablonski have to say for himself, then?"

"Don't know, really. Seems like Pomme makes him laugh. Come on up!"

Zed extended his arm to show them the way.

Carmen took hold of it. "I was just wanting to say . . . thanks for the dictionaries."

"Oh . . . that was nothing."

"No. It's really a swell gift."

And with that, Carmen pulled Zed closer and kissed him on the cheek. Terry leaned over and did likewise on Zed's other cheek.

That night, Lionel Arsenault dreamed he was waiting for someone, for a business meeting, in a restaurant in the Old Quarter of New Orleans. It was as though he knew the city well, even though he did not live there. And the staff waited on him with that mixture of attention and ease usually reserved for regular customers. But, instead of the business people he was expecting, it was Sylvia who showed up, wearing a panama hat. Lionel was doubly surprised.

"You bought a hat, then?"

Sylvia shrugged. "I was killing time."

Sylvia's reply shook him. There was no trace of reproach in her tone, but the phrase seemed brutal and full of some darker meaning.

"Really? It's the first time I've heard you say that."

Sylvia laughed. "It's also the first time I buy little cigars. Would you like one?"

"Comme . . . what would have happened, do you suppose, if Hitler had been accepted at that fine arts college? And why wasn't he accepted? Qui décide what's art and what isn't? Or who's got talent and who hasn't?"

No one, not Zed, nor Terry, nor Carmen, nor Lisa-M., had ever seen Pomme in such a state. He was tossing out questions without waiting for them to land. Even Étienne and Ludmilla seemed to take pleasure in seeing them floating all around them.

"If you ask me, I don't see how art can communicate universally. Même que the whole idea of communicating doesn't make much sense, does it. You ask me, communication is highly overrated. Art talks to art. It's like books, really. They talk back and forth to one another."

". . ."

Terry tried to imagine how books talked to one another.

Pomme was well aware that his discourse was a bit all over the place, but only a bit. "They talk about l'émotion artistique; is that sort of émotion something you learn, or what? Ask me, I'd say 90 percent of the time there's nothing naturel about it. And I'm being generous."

A moment of silence ensued, so brief that no one had time to break it before Pomme launched into a kind of conclusion. "I wouldn't mind being le Leo Castelli d'Acadie! Ou maybe his assistant, au moins . . ."

All things considered, Zed decided that Pomme was in fine form and deserved a toast. "Sounds good to me. Leo Castelli . . . santé!"

The others followed his lead willingly. Raising his glass, Terry realized that the divination "Before Completion" was coming true.

Ludmilla turned to Terry to inquire after little Étienne.

"Woman lives downstairs didn't mind sleeping up in our place. She's done it before a couple of times."

"That's awfully nice of her."

"Oh . . . we pay her. Well, I suppose it's nice just the same. I mean, helps us out, it does. Really."

Nice. The word had come out in English. But Terry had almost caught it. Better still, he'd avoided saying that the woman "ne mindait pas," a phrase that would normally have come tumbling out. He turned to Carmen a bit sheepishly. "I suppose I've got to get used to it."

"Sure. I've got to catch myself sometimes as well, don't you know."

40.

XIE / DELIVERANCE

"I'm expecting to work on the Petitcodiac up until the end of August. As a rule, that's when they start letting folks go."

Terry's dad looked at his son, amazed at how different he was from his other children. True, he was the youngest of the lot.

"At first, Carmen and I were thinking we'd work together in the bar. Afterwards, we thought this way would be a whole lot better."

Terry's dad listened. Unformulated questions — if such things were possible — were crashing about in his head. At last, the words came together. "Yes . . . but a bookstore, as you say . . . I mean, do you know anything about that sort of business?"

"Not that much, I suppose, but I tell myself, with Ludmilla there . . . I mean, between the two of us, I'm sure we'll manage."

". . ."

"We won't be paying any rent the first year, on account of we'll be staying in the building. It's kind of a way to help us out. The place is a sort of co-op, did I tell you?"

". . ."

"Carmen'll be working with Josse. They work well together as it is and, well, now it'll truly be theirs, won't it. The business, I mean."

". . ."

"They've got some not-so-bad ideas, they do."

". . ."

"And you remember Pomme, don't you?"

". . . ?"

"Anyhow, him and Zablonski are opening an art gallery. And there'll be a restaurant as well, and a couple of stores. It's all starting to fall into place."

". . ."

"You wouldn't have to lend me the money directly. You'd only be signing for me at the bank."

". . ."

"Carmen's dad said he'd sign for the both of us but, well, I'd prefer if it came from our side as well. It'd be more equal, I suppose."

It had been a long time since Lionel Arsenault had taken a day off to hang around the house. His decision had surprised even Sylvia.

"I feel like making us a grand supper. We might invite some guests."

In Sylvia's mind, the idea of doing such a thing on a Tuesday was unusual, to say the least.

Having searched through their recipe books, Lionel Arsenault had proposed either a paella or his specialty, a dune clam pie.

"As you like. Both are fine."

"I suppose it depends what I'll find over at Melanson's. I'll go over there later."

Sylvia had not finished her housework. She wondered if she ought to interrupt it to start making invitations.

"Who is it you're thinking we ought to invite, then?"

Lionel finished reading an article in the newspaper before replying, as he turned the page, "Don't know, really . . . It's been a while since we saw our neighbours, seems to me."

"I knew from the start he'd say yes. It was just his way of listening that was, well . . . I don't know . . . it was like something else was going on in his head the whole time."

". . ."

"As though he wasn't really listening but thinking about something else at the same time. Well, not just anything, mind you . . ."

"You ought to have asked him, if it's bothering you so very much."

"I didn't know it was going to bother me, did I. And bother might be too strong a word. I suppose I'm more like intrigued than bothered, really."

It made Carmen happy to hear Terry use a word like "intrigué," but Terry was too busy extricating the whistle from Étienne's mouth to realize it.

"At what age does a child learn to whizzle in a whizzler, anyhow?"

"Don't know, do I. There's no hurry, far as I'm concerned."

Terry bounced Étienne on his knees to make him forget the whistle, while Carmen finished preparing supper.

"You ought to ask your dad's advice. After all, he's had his business all his life. Might be he could give you some pointers. And you might be able to find out what it is he's really thinking."

Terry thought a moment. "I'm not so sure I want to know what it is he's really thinking."

Carmen opened the oven door and slid in the dish of lasagna, which was ready for baking at last.

"Does the future scare you at all? What we've gotten ourselves into, I mean."

"Sometimes."

Carmen leaned back against the counter for a moment, crossed her hands over her large belly, and explained, "Well, to be honest, most times, it's exciting. Don't know what it is lately — might be this thing with the lofts and all — but it's like we're not alone. Oh, there'll always be little difficulties, I expect, this and that. But I don't really see them as problems."

Then, because she'd kind of surprised herself, she added thoughtfully, "Hmm!"

Terry was full of admiration. He said nothing until they were seated at the table. "You're right. I believe I's going to ask Dad what he's really thinking."

"I am going to ask," Carmen corrected.

Terry repeated: "I am."

". . ."

"Well, admit it, there's some mistakes that just make sense! I am, you are, he is . . . It's not all that well thought out, you ask me. These days, some fellow in marketing would lose his job if he suggested something like that!"

"We're calling it a galerie d'art, but it's not really that. It's a whole lot more. Fact is, the gallery's the least of it."

Lisa-M. had not been going out with Pomme for long, but that didn't make her shy. "You ask me, you're in denial."

Pomme took it with good humour. "See, the idea's not to sell, not even to show. That's just the obvious part. And it isn't to do Duchamp all over again either, or even Warhol. That's comme another level. The network and all that. We're looking for a third level, maybe even a fourth."

Lisa-M. had her practical side. "And what for, then?"

The question caught Pomme by surprise.

Lisa-M. rephrased it. "I don't know why you're trying so hard for something else . . . Folks are still quite happy with the Impressionists."

Pomme agreed. "Well, it's just that . . . the third level — let's call it that — is very close. Very, very close. It's in the air. We can't see it yet, but it'll show itself before too long. Can't do otherwise, can it."

Lisa-M. was impressed by Pomme's conviction, although she still had her doubts. "And you think it'll be showing itself here? In Moncton, I mean?"

Pomme welcomed the question, because it allowed him, at last, to say what he truly felt: "I do."

The response was unequivocal.

". . ."

". . ."

"And Zablonski thinks so as well?"

"Zablonski's working on some new things. That's all I'm asking of him, for now."

Little Étienne was barely out the door with his grandmother Després when Terry seized the vacuum cleaner — aspirateur-traineau, if you please — and began a major cleanup of the apartment: not quite what is generally referred to as a spring cleaning, but a good end-of-winter cleanup, at least. He displaced many more things than usual as he pushed the rug-and-floor brush — le suceur?! — putting into boxes those things that were no longer useful and would most probably not survive the move to the loft. He worked with the same joyful energy with which the sun's rays and the fresh spring air poured through the open windows of the apartment. Carmen's confidence had given him wings, not to mention his most recent Yi Jing reading, which predicted nothing less than complete deliverance, and without the slightest equivocation.

Hexagram 40 spoke of renewed energy, of a liberation, *great good fortune, in complete accord with the forces of the universe.* In other words, the Way had never been so open. According to the French manual — often, Terry had to admit, more passionate than the others — this was the hexagram of the great heights, of the dramatic finale, the heroic situation, and miraculous deliverance.

At that very moment, as he was pushing the rug-and-floor brush near the chest of drawers, Terry's elbow knocked over the little bowl containing his divination marbles. He turned off the machine to gather the marbles and tidy up the chest. When he counted them to make sure he'd found them all, Terry realized there were seventeen instead of sixteen. He recounted them, checked his books to be sure. There was no mistake: from the beginning, he'd been working with one too many marbles.

Zed's father had been awarded a small contract to do some work in the lofts. Zed was watching him work.

"It'll have to be checked souvent. An old building like this, there's toujours one thing or another that might go."

Zed agreed.

His father dropped one tool to pick up another. "Well, I suppose it'll last as long as it lasts."

". . ."

"Those big cathedrals and old castles over in Europe, they must cost a pretty penny to keep up. I wonder who it is that pays for all that."

". . ."

"See this joint, here? Really, it oughtn't to have been done like this. They ought to have turned it par là and then drawn it par en bas. But it's the best they could do, à cause de l'autre pipe là."

". . ."

"Quand même, it's pretty solid. Ought to hold up."

". . ."

"Sometimes, même si it's not by the book, it can work pareil."

". . ."

"Have you picked out your loft, then?"

"Not yet. I suppose I'm waiting for the end, or close to. I'll take whatever's left."

His father cast a suspicious eye on Zed, without stopping his work. "You know best, I suppose. Des fois, there's nothing wrong with leftovers."

Terry had not been able to keep from phoning Carmen to tell her about the extra marble. "No, but I can hardly believe it! The very basis of the whole thing was off right from the start!" Terry had used the English "off," but, this being an emergency, he'd made no effort to correct himself.

Carmen, on the other hand, had very different concerns. "The fellow from Moosehead Beer is here. I want to talk to him about our bar. Can you tell me about your marbles tonight?"

Terry did not feel offended. "No problem. Anyhow, I expect it'll take me weeks to figure out what it all means."

The light lingers later every evening in Étienne and Ludmilla's make-do apartment. Sitting near a window, Étienne is drawing on a scrap of cardboard he picked up somewhere. He is more absorbed than usual in his scribbling. Lines flourish, go off in all directions, and yet a kind of order reigns. As in a kind of dance.

"Étienne?"

"Yes?"

Having found her husband in this space that's constantly changing with the latest renovations, Ludmilla moves up behind him. "What are you doing?"

Étienne shows her the drawing. "Why?"

"No reason. I was just wondering what you were up to. You didn't seem to be reading."

Terry was washing the dishes; Carmen was drying.

"It's as though different keys could unlock the same door."

Carmen did not find this possibility particularly surprising. "Well, a skeleton key can open a bunch of doors, can't it? I'd say it's pretty much the same thing."

Terry followed his line of reasoning to its logical conclusion. "Not if we're talking about the doors to two different cars: say one car works fine, while the other's got no brakes." Terry had used the English word "brakes."

"Freins," Carmen corrected.

"Freins," Terry repeated.

Terry was scraping the lasagna dish, which had been reheated twice. He knew his reasoning was unclear. And yet, he was convinced he'd glimpsed some new slice of reality. "All right, then, say it was like you were listening to two different CDs. Say one's Dylan, the other's Cohen. And both CDs put you in the exact same mood." He used the English word "mood."

Carmen was being patient, although she hoped this discussion would not go on all evening. "If that's the case, I'd say your mood" — she too used the English word — "your mood's got less to do with the music, and more to do with you."

Terry let the glass dish slide into the sink and raised his arms to exclaim, "That's it! That's exactly it! That's what I've been seeing, except that, now, I understand it differently."

"Anyhow, a mood — I suppose we ought to say humeur — is nothing fixed, is it. Kind of hard to compare it to a car."

"Exactly. There's that part as well. Reality isn't fixed either, now, is it? Matter of fact, I'm starting to believe that reality — I mean, what we call reality — doesn't exist at all. It's something altogether different."

"And who, pray tell, would know what it is, then?"

Terry fished out the dish from the bottom of the sink where it had settled. "That's the big question, isn't it."

". . ."

". . ."

". . ."

Finally, Terry felt unable to say more. He imagined the big question playing hide-and-seek somewhere up behind the clouds. He decided to let it play on.

Later, in bed, after one or two fumbling attempts to harmonize their yin and yang, Terry and Carmen lay wrapped in each other's arms.

"It's not all that serious, really. It's only a . . . how is it you say 'yield' in French?"

"Cédez."

"It's really only a cédez. We end up merging just the same. How do you say 'merging'?"

Carmen wasn't sure.

"Remind me to look that word up tomorrow, won't you?"

Carmen had reached the edge of sleep.

"You do know I'll love you till the day I die, don't you?"

Instead of speaking, Carmen squeezed his forearm, holding it for several long seconds. It was, Terry felt, a fine answer.